THE BEAST OF DEATH CAVERN

A NOVEL BY MICHAEL COLE

THE BEAST OF DEATH CAVERN

WWW.SEVEREDPRESS.COM

ISBN: 978-1-923165-79-3

CHAPTER 1

Roland Welker thought the cold would numb the pain. In reality, it made the firing nerves all the more intense, and definitely noticeable.

He rolled onto his back and examined his rifle. There was plenty of ammo, not that it mattered. Blaster bolts, designed to tear through standard light infantry armor, failed to penetrate his attacker's hide. Who would ever guess white fur was stronger than Nile-grade infantry battle suits?

Welker looked to the sky. There was maybe one more hour of light remaining. It was safe to assume the enormous humanoid was not scared of the dark. If Welker was eighteen feet tall and equally as ferocious, he wouldn't be either. But the fact was that he was a puny human; fragile, soft, and not nearly as ferocious as he thought he was just minutes ago.

Aguret was a planet which had once been the crown jewel of its star system. Perfectly spaced from its star at ninety-two million miles, it had oceans, lakes, large plains, forests, and a thriving ecosystem. But all of that changed when a passing meteorite with a mass doubling Aguret's sped through the system. Gravity sucked the planet out of its regular orbit, instantly plunging it into a winter that endured for the twenty-thousand years following the event.

Not all life was eradicated. Some small animals adapted to life on the forest floors. Even the flora adapted, their roots managing to get moisture from the frozen ground. But, for the most part, Aguret was not teeming with life. What little there was usually cowered in the presence of the invasive human species that occupied a small area on the west hemisphere.

That is, until today.

Welker stared at the red snow under his leg. It was extremely bright. He always thought of blood as dark, but something about it in the snow made it seem as bright as highlighter ink. The beast had only nicked him, and yet, his flesh was severely lacerated. Bad enough that, if he did not act quickly, he would bleed out.

Rifle shots popped off somewhere behind the trees. A growl rumbled in response, followed by a tremor of intense motion. The shooting stopped and a howling scream began.

Welker knew the voice. It was Jerry Asfelt. The poor guy had been cursed with a last name that made him the target of many jokes, and a hilarious nickname of "ass-felt." He took it well and laughed at himself along with everyone else.

Right now, he wasn't laughing. Nor would he for what would hopefully be the last few seconds of life he had left.

He had seen the way the thing had handled the team leader, Rhanda. It tore off all four of his limbs, taking its time with each one. It seemed fascinated by the agony it caused, as well as the horror experienced by the rest of the squad who could do nothing but watch.

Judging by the pitches and rhythm of Jerry Asfelt's screaming, he was suffering a similar fate.

Welker tried steadying his hands while applying his tourniquet to his leg, all the while watching the direction of his fellow soldier's agony. The trees and uneven landscape blocked his view. Maybe it was for the best. It was not as if he needed to witness Jerry's fate.

He reached into his medpack and dug out a stapler. It was a painful, but necessary process. Two clips, and the laceration was mostly sealed. Next, he sprayed some liquid sealant onto the wound. Fortunately, it was enough to stop the bleeding for now.

After wrapping his leg as best he could, Welker scooted back. His basic field dressing was precisely that: basic. It would only serve him in the short term. By the sounds of it, all he may have accomplished was prolonging his misery. He was still stuck out here in the cold.

After what felt like an eternity, he came near a towering rock structure called Sleeping Ridge; essentially a hundred-and-fifty-foot piece of rock which crested westwards like a tidal wave. He settled on the narrowest point, where the top was only ten feet high. There, Welker double-checked his field dressing, then leaned back and waited.

Waiting was all he could do. His leg kept him from trekking back to the outpost. Nobody was around to help him, as Jerry was the last of his squad. The speeders were wrecked. His radio was trashed. Nobody knew he was out here.

All he could do was wait and hope for the best. And be sure to put a round through his skull in the event he was discovered by the beast.

CHAPTER 2

"Let's pick up the pace, fellas. Dragging ass only delays the inevitable. It's our turn to answer the call of duty."

Sergeant Austin Naray gave a glance to the LT. Skerrit was speaking to himself just as much as the five men under his command. Though he didn't say it outright, he could not blame the troops for taking their time. Outpost duty was either loved or dreaded. For most people, it was the latter.

The assignment was three straight weeks of nothing. It served as both a research station and part of the Pine Tree radar system. It was all meant to create an interplanetary network of detection systems in the system dividing the Legacy Union and the newer and more rebellious New Age Coalition.

Since the New Age Revolution forty Earth years ago, in which the new territories declared their independence from what was now called Legacy, tensions and paranoia was rampant within the government. Even though there was hardly a shot fired between the two factions, there were a few hot moments involving a standoff between heavily armed fleets at the border.

Both sides had essentially agreed to leave each other alone, but Legacy was wary of sneak attacks.

New Age lacked the weapons and ships for an invasion, but all the same, the planetary governments running Legacy used them as a boogeyman for endless military spending.

For the radar system to work, there needed to be several stations located throughout each planet that bordered the neutral zone. There were a few central bases on each of those planets, where drills were regularly conducted, ships were maintained, and troops were deployed in the event of suspicious activity. Drug smugglers on private freighters, as well as pirates and human traffickers, were always on the move. The latter two were generally the type to put up a fight when boarded; something Naray and his fellow troops appreciated. They did not undergo the grueling training regiment for nothing. And, for better or worse, there was plenty of criminal strongholds that needed to be smoked out in the quadrant.

But outpost duty was the polar opposite. Out there, they were babysitting a radar dish and, in this case, science nerds.

Scientific research was an ongoing trade that would last as long as the human species did. Naray couldn't truly hold anything against it; research was what led to interstellar travel, vaccines which enabled humans to coexist with alien flora and fauna, and so much more. Scientists were just a different personality type than the military personnel. Not all were bad, but many of them were pompous individuals who saw themselves as intellectually superior to the "meatheads", despite overwhelmingly depending on those same "meatheads" for safety, utilities, and transportation.

"Let's go, gentlemen. Jesus, you're like a bunch of horny high-schoolers. You're not heading out to war, guys. Let's move it along."

Now, Lieutenant Skerrit was genuinely sounding impatient.

"Come on, fellas," Naray said. "Alpha Team won't take kindly to us being late. Neither will colony administration, so let's move it."

He tapped his boot against the boarding ramp for their transport. It was a forty-year-old gunship, long retired from combat duty, and now relegated to shuttling staff from point A to point B. Bullet craters and carbon scoring decorated its hull. The twin rotors had a mild squeaky sound whenever they began rotating, and always had the passengers nervous throughout the trip.

It was probably reason eight-hundred-and-ninety-nine why the men took their sweet time. Regardless, they broke away from whatever they were doing and began making their way for the gunship.

Except for Pedro. He was still busy making out with what's-her-name. It was always a different woman. The guy was at risk of going through the entire colony at this rate. And for some reason, the females went with it. Even some of the married ones. Probably it was a good thing the man-whore was moving a thousand miles north. It was only a matter of time before at least one of the husbands figured out what he was doing. There hadn't been a murder on this planet yet. At the rate Pedro was going, it almost seemed as if he was eager to be the first victim.

"How he can do that in the blazing cold is beyond me," Badejo said. Contrary to regulations, he had two inches of growth on his face. The bitter cold on this planet made shaving a real hassle. Even in the warmth of the facilities, the hairs seemed thicker and more rigid, and the skin more susceptible to cuts.

Naray brushed a large snowflake off his nose.

"Looks like he's keeping warm to me."

Standing a few feet behind Badejo was Corporal Dodger. It was a name that earned a wide range of jokes, both in training exercises, sports, and bad relationships. 'Dodging bullets left and right,' everyone would say. Living up to that name, he was a spry soldier who made good use of the colony's gymnasium. Back home, he was a marathon runner and enjoyed sports such as soccer. Here on Aguret, everyone naturally signed him up for dodgeball. Of course. Much to their delight, he was always hard to hit.

He followed Badejo up the ramp. "Why the hell do they need a whole squad to occupy one little tin can?"

"Company property," Naray replied in a matter-of-fact tone. Anything owned or provided by the Union-Space Corporation, the military's number one contractor, was considered high-value.

Last, but not least, was Waterstan. The team medic, he rejected the title of nurse, despite being fully registered. It was not as though he was ashamed of the profession, but needless to say, this group of meatheads had a way of feminizing the term when addressing him.

Demonstrating this fact was their gunship pilot, Angelo. "Oh Nuuuurse!"

Waterstan groaned. "What?"

"I made sure to get those painkillers you ordered on our manifest," Angelo replied.

Waterstan widened his eyes and nodded in shocked approval. He actually got an intelligent answer from the guy. Miracles never ceased.

"Excellent," he said.

Naray equally approved, both of the delivery and the message itself. He agreed with the medic that the outposts were poorly supplied. For a company and government that talked a big game of how it spared no expense, they certainly liked to cut corners when it came to their soldiers and field equipment. The 'spare no expense' part really came into play regarding their corporate and government offices. The little people—the people like Naray and his teammates—had to put up with poorly insulated metal walls and value-brand coffee.

"Pedro! Get your ass over here!" he called to the straggling soldier.

Pedro pried his face from his date and began moving towards the ship. "Sorry baby, I gotta go."

"Call me every day," she said, hands over her heart.

"I promise! See you when I get back!" Pedro blew a kiss, then hustled to the gunship.

Naray closed his eyes and exhaled slowly, simultaneously amused and repulsed by his act, as well as the woman's gullibility. She actually thought she had a shot at making an honest man out of Pedro. That, and she was somehow unaware of his reputation.

With all the men aboard, Skerrit took his seat, leaving the sergeant to close the ramp. Naray hit the lift button. The gears did their little whine and the metal slab came out of the snow. It rose two feet, then came to an abrupt stop. The gears clanged and clunked, forcing Naray to quickly stop the lift.

"Oh, great."

"What'd you do?" Angelo called to him.

"Don't even think about blaming me," Naray said. "These birds are not meant to operate in a winter climate for long periods of time."

"Same with me," Waterstan muttered. He had a tissue to his nose.

The rest of the group chuckled at his expense. The sight of their medic catching his hundredth cold was not something that inspired confidence.

The pilot stepped out of the cockpit and moved through the fuselage of the aircraft. Like most people on this planet, he was a few pounds overweight. It was hard to keep in shape when living long-term in a place like this. It was always snowing, the temperature was twenty degrees on a good day, and the colony's gym was small and always crowded. On top of that, crew quarters were small, not allowing for much activity or movement. Turning into a slob was almost inevitable.

Angelo stepped outside and removed a panel on the ship to provide a visual of the gears. "Yep, just as I thought. Iced up. Hang on." He moved to a compartment on the starboard side and pulled out a thin cannister with a small hose protruding from the top. He pointed the nozzle at the gears and coated the ice with blue fluid called rapid antifreeze. "Alright, Sarge. Give it another try."

Naray hit the button again. The gears did their whining as they lifted the ramp. It lifted to eighty degrees and slammed home.

"Ramp's secure."

He took his seat.

Angelo reentered the cockpit through the forward entrance. "Keep all hands and feet in the vehicle."

A dull cranking sound from both rotors made all of the passengers, including Lieutenant Skerrit, wince.

The gunship lifted off the icy ground and ascended above the trees.

For a moment, Naray was able to get a bird's-eye view of the colony. With a name like Crown Station, one would think the place would have a grand design like a castle. On the contrary, the colony was a horseshoe-shaped set of modules comprised of galvanized steel, with a separate power plant half a mile to the south and a fueling garage near the 'bend'. A few vehicles and staff moved about, performing their routine tasks. Life here on Aguret was exactly that: routine.

It was why Naray was unbothered by the assignment to Station Four. If anything, the crew quarters were actually better. They were larger, and everyone had one for themselves, as the modules were originally designed to hold nearly thirty science staff.

Speaking of the staff…

Naray looked to the lieutenant. "I see it's just us. Not delivering any nerds to the station?"

"Negative," Skerrit replied. "There are four science staff on site. According to the log, they're out investigating the aftereffects of the recent quake that shook up the mountain."

"Yeah, I heard a big chasm opened up in the mountainside," Pedro said.

"Something like that," Skerrit said. "Anyway, they determined the mountain is stable enough to get a look at the thing. So, they're off-station for a couple of days. Meaning we'll have the outpost to ourselves for the first twenty-four hours or so."

That was of no nevermind to Naray. The science staff typically didn't mingle with the soldiers anyway.

"Any updates from Alpha Team?" he asked.

"Negative," Skerrit said with a slightly puzzled look on his face. "The last log was put in almost twelve hours ago. Just a standard routine maintenance check of the dish. After that, nothing."

Naray shrugged it off. "Gives us an opportunity to give their LT shit when we get there."

Skerrit looked out the window, his professional veneer cracking momentarily. "At least that's something for us to do."

CHAPTER 3

"This is amazing. Absolutely amazing."

Dr. Toby Anderson almost appeared possessed as he looked over the huge skeletal remains. The expedition to the edge of the chasm proved more than worth it. They thought they would get a look at various layers of granite and maybe discover some mineral deposits. Such things would probably prove more beneficial to Crown Station at large.

But this find was cooler, and was far more likely to get him recognition in the field of science.

Sasha Serigami could already envision the headlines. Geologist discovers remains of reptilian species on a frozen snow planet. A graduate student, she too was fascinated by the discovery. But she was fascinated because she was invested in the benefits of research and discovery. Not becoming a celebrity.

Toby Anderson was a man in his late forties, though he looked over a decade older than that. A lifetime of stress had a way of aging someone. Sasha was twenty-seven and had only been under his wing for a year, all of which was off-world. It was enough time to get a read on his personality and history; the former demonstrated by the professor himself on a daily basis and the latter given to Sasha by other students and staff who had worked with him much longer.

Like most non-military staff on the planet, Toby was unshaven. His five days of growth was greying and patchy. When he wasn't wearing a thick scarf and hood, he sported a safari hat, as though he considered himself a grand adventurer. Others studying geology and glaciers on the planet spilled the beans to Sasha that an *Indiana Jones* type was always how Toby envisioned himself. Since his teen years, he sported the hat. But he was anything but similar to the characters he idolized. He was not athletic, nor did he have the charm. On this planet, he tried to keep fieldwork to under a day in duration; that way he would not have to set up camp, and instead return to the relative comforts of the outpost or Crown Station.

This was the one exception where he had no intention of going back. At least, not until they had catalogued as much information as possible. After all, he had discovered a new species.

Technically, Sasha was the one who saw the crocodilian jaws first, and identified the rest of the creature's enormous bulk covered in snow and ice. But, needless to say, Toby would take credit, as he was the one in charge. Somehow, she knew the guy would not credit her for the initial find.

"Amazing indeed," a shivering George Morty said. He completed the measurement requested by the doctor. "Standing upright, it probably reached a height of thirteen feet."

"It definitely stood on its hind legs," Beth Kruse said. Both she and George were glaciology majors, and visibly unnerved by the huge teeth in the dead creature's mouth. A snap of those jaws could easily tear an adult human in half. And this was no fossil. This was a creature that had recently died.

Up until now, it was thought only small critters lived on Aguret. Not only was this a large animal, but it was unlike anything that would typically live in this type of environment. Its skin was textured like that of a snake. Its back held three columns of spines, the center rising eight inches high and cresting in the direction of its tail.

In length, it was maybe twenty feet. George had made the measurement, but Sasha didn't catch it thanks to a gust of wind. Her thoughts mirrored Beth's concerns. They were unspoken, but they were still clear as day thanks to the look on her face and the way she repeatedly watched their surroundings.

It was something Sasha was willing to bring voice to.

"Doctor?"

Toby was kneeling by the animal's forearms, not even bothering to give her eye contact. "Yes?"

"It's a great find, yes. But we might want to report back to the outpost."

Now, he was looking at her. "And why would we want to do that?"

"Where there's one, there's another," Sasha explained. "This thing is no fossil. It died recently, and judging by the way the skin on its neck is torn, it was not from old age."

George stepped away, having taken notice of the fatal injury. Like Toby, he was so taken by the very sight of the thing that it did not dawn on his mind as to *why* it was dead in the first place.

"Holy crap! Something killed it."

"That's my point," Sasha said. "Where there's one, there's another. Maybe not the same animal, but equally as violent."

Toby took some new images of the corpse. He had heard her words, but as though caught in the annoying breeze, they had blown away.

"This had to have come from the cavern," he said. He looked to the north. "That earthquake opened up a gold mine. We might have access to new resources *and* an entirely unique ecosystem."

"One where dinosaurs exist?" Beth said through chattering teeth. "How can something like this exist here?"

"Must be warm-blooded, for starters," Toby said. "Maybe it lived during the planet's original cycle, then evolved to adapt to the cool temperatures."

"The cavern might have provided it protection as well," Sasha suggested. She had her arms wrapped around herself. Her thermal coat, sweaters, scarf, and hoodie were not enough against this endless winter. She swore that once she got her PhD, she would only work on warm worlds. The only thing worse than this would be endless humidity, like the swamp planet Yekota. Thankfully, there was not much work in her field being done there.

"So, you think this thing was cut off from the valley?" George asked.

"The cavern probably cuts through the entire mountain," Toby said, growing more excited. "We haven't been able to explore the opposite side. There could be all sorts of animal life."

"Very true, and very concerning," Sasha said. "I really don't want to become lunch."

Toby tucked his camera back into his pack, then put it on his back. "Quit worrying. This is science, Sasha. Opportunities like this do not present themselves every day. In fact, they're extraordinarily rare. To pack up and leave right at the dawn of discovery…" he shook his head, "…all I can say is good luck getting future grants."

"I'm not saying abandon the site," Sasha replied, her voice barely concealing her moral outrage. "All I'm suggesting is we come out here while better prepared. Probably with the soldiers escorting us, which we should've had a couple of them tag along to begin with."

Toby scoffed at the very mention of the military.

"Yeah, sure." He gave another look at the beast. Its forelimbs were tucked close to its chest, their claws half coiled as though digging into an invisible foe.

The doctor squinted, then took a knee by the huge black nails. He pried something from the tip of one of them, then held it in the grey natural light of the sun's rays beaming through the clouds.

Sasha leaned in to see through the flakes of snow. It was a patch of white hair.

"Well, hot damn."

"Definitely not from a reptile," Toby said. "This came from a mammal. This is long hair, too. No way this came from one of the little rodents. I believe this came off something at least as big as this fella."

Now, everyone was watching their surroundings. The storm had only started a few hours ago. Any tracks that the animal may have left would have been coated by the snow. Branches snapped and marred the thick layer of snow on the earth, further preventing them from identifying the direction the reptile's killer had gone.

"I think Sasha's right," Beth said. "We don't know what else may be out here. Let's get better prepared and come back. Preferably with an armed escort."

Toby scoffed again. The usual look of intellectual superiority took full form on his face. Maybe it was the wind or a shred of common sense… or a lack of willpower to continue arguing with his assistants—but he refrained from condescending remarks. He checked his watch and his personal tablet.

"Sasha, when was the last time you tried contacting the guys at the outpost?"

"A few minutes ago," she replied. It was strange. It was entirely unlike the soldiers to not answer calls. Even before the storm, the outpost went silent. Initially, the group brushed it off as equipment failure or the lieutenant being on the john. Dumb theories, but they considered it an unimportant matter at the time.

But now, they had discovered something the soldiers should be warned about.

"Alright, you guys win," Toby said. "We'll head west towards Sleeping Ridge. The trees from here to there are thickly grouped enough to keep the snow passable for our Cruiser. Pack up the shelter and we'll head back. And don't forget the samples."

The team went right to work. Nothing motivated Sasha and her colleagues more than the promise of four walls and coffee. That, and not being out in the woods while something that killed an alien dinosaur was lurking.

CHAPTER 4

After six hours of flight time, the ride started getting bumpy. A cold front was moving down from the north and coating the entire area with snow. On a winter planet like Aguret, this was nothing new. The only anomaly was the fact that it swept south faster than was initially forecasted. Otherwise, they would have departed earlier.

For the next hour, the squad of soldiers jittered in their seats, watching streaks of snow zipping past their windows like shooting stars and listening to their pilot make his millionth attempt to make contact with Alpha Team.

"*Green Line* to Outpost Four, please respond… Son of a bitch."

"Still nothing?" Lieutenant Skerrit asked.

"Never had this happen before," Angelo said. "The only thing that makes sense is that the storm is causing interference. That, or maybe there's been some damage to the tower."

The second theory made enough sense. Like most other items, the radio tower was not designed for endless winter. It constantly needed winterizing, and sometimes the staff either lacked the supplies or the proper safety gear to tend to do the work.

Naray leaned back and closed his eyes. It would not be long before they set down. Angelo would refuel and do some other ground maintenance, Alpha Team would pass along any information, and then board the gunship and head for Crown Station.

After a flight like this, it would be tempting to plop down in a bunk and snooze. Naray, being a sergeant, reminded himself to give assignments to the men based on the state of the outpost. There always needed to be somebody on watch, and regular inspections of the dish needed to be made. That, and there was no guarantee the galley and other areas would be clean. In the days leading up to a rotation, outpost staff were more focused on packing up and getting the private quarters in order. As a result, the rest of the station was not given much attention.

On the plus side, some of the guys got some snoozing in during the flight. Good for them, bad for Naray. Their snoring was like nails on a chalkboard. The guilty parties would definitely get the least desirable assignments.

"Alright, we're nearing your home for the next two months," Angelo announced.

Skerrit put away his tablet and sat up straight. "You heard him, men. Wake up. Get ready for work."

"Oh, yay," Waterstan remarked.

Everyone strapped themselves in for the descent. Everyone except Pedro, who was distracted with his personal tablet.

"Hey!" Naray barked at him.

"Huh?" Pedro looked at him, then had an 'oh!' moment. He typed something on his device, then clipped his seat harness.

"What's going on there, Pedro?"

"Uh, nothing!"

The private first-class' shy response got the attention of everyone aboard the flight, including Angelo.

"Uh-oh!" Dodger said. "This has got to be good. Maybe it's a stalker."

"Nah," Badejo replied. "That'd get him excited."

"Ugly stalker then!" Dodger said with a raised finger.

"Will you all shut up?" Pedro said.

Even Naray and Skerrit were grinning. They had never seen Pedro like this. All at once, he had a glow, yet looked sicker than ever.

Naray shifted to get a glance at his tablet screen. It was a personal message window, with a picture of the woman he was making out with on the top of the screen.

"Maybe Dodger's right about the stalker," he said with a laugh.

"What's she saying?" Skerrit asked, triggering laughter from the others.

Badejo formed a heart shape with his hands and exaggerated a woman's voice. "I love you, Pedro. Come home to me."

"Yeah, yeah, shut up," Pedro groaned.

He was trying to come off as laughing with the group, but was still looking pale. The change in air pressure was probably not helping matters.

"She probably thinks she can make an honest man out of him," Skerrit said.

"Some people think they can win the lottery too," Badejo replied. He tilted his head, perplexed at his own statement. "Wait… I just compared Pedro to the lottery…"

Dodger leaned forward and snatched the tablet from the side pocket of Pedro's seat. The soldier whipped to his right to stop the eavesdropper.

"Hey!"

Chuckling mischievously, Dodger scrolled through the conversation between Pedro and the woman.

"Wow… Her name's January."

"Perfect name for someone living here," Waterstan quipped.

Dodger continued scrolling. "Whoa!" He beamed a smile at Pedro. "Congratulations… and my condolences."

"I knew it," Skerrit said. "She wants to go steady with him."

"Well, yeah," Dodger said. "That's all true. But that's the least of Pedro's worries."

Everyone read between the lines.

"Oh, shit!" Waterstan said. "He knocked her up, didn't he?"

Dodger handed the tablet back to a shrunken-looking Pedro. "Yep!"

The gunship filled with laughter and some whooping. Pedro looked like a zombie, still absorbing the information Dodger was now broadcasting to the whole ship.

Naray had seen the same look in his older brother. Fear, anxiety, excitement, guilt, and a hundred other emotions were forming a nasty cocktail that made the soldier look as though he would expel something.

"She was going to tell me after I got back from outpost duty." Pedro switched the device off. "I guess she couldn't hold off."

"She's madly in love," Dodger said with glee. "She's already longing for her man, and it's only been seven hours. And she's glowing like a star. Decided she couldn't wait for him to get back."

"Oh, geez," Waterstan said. "If only she knew."

"Knew what?" Pedro said.

Everyone laughed at the question.

"Are you serious?" Dodger said. "Your reputation is so well known, I'm surprised it's not a documentary. January is apparently the only one who doesn't know."

"No, she knows," Pedro said. "Our first time was, um…" His shyness vanished for a moment, and the Pedro everyone knew resurfaced. "Mmm…"

Waterstan grimaced, having put the pieces together. "Wait… you, her, *and...*"

"Threesome." Naray shrugged. "Not sure if I'm feeling critical or impressed. At least we know she's open-minded."

"She's definitely not boring," Skerrit remarked.

"Well, mazel tov," Naray said, lifting his hand as though to give a toast.

"First thing's first," Angelo called back to them. "We're eight hundred meters out, turning on final."

CHAPTER 5

As the dropship approached the southeast side of Outpost Four, the passengers were able to get a clear visual through their windows. Firstly, they saw the massive radar dish protruding from the middle of the compound. It stood on a large tower, the dish pointed upward and expanded to its full two-hundred-foot width.

The compound itself was designed to be modular. Four large steel walls served as a large barrier between the modules and the outside world. If it had been dome-shaped, that would have made a difference. At various points in the walls were guard posts overlooking the outside. Each one had a Kraken-V3 turret installed, capable of firing a concentrated stream of plasma energy at an oncoming target, or be used for rapid fire. In normal conditions, they were fully reliable. After two years being smothered in ice? Only the northeast and the center west guns were still operational. They had been heavily used, and in the mind of Legacy, they had served their purpose. It was protocol to have guns on every outpost. For the Legacy military, this was their way of saving costs and discarding useless equipment. It was not as though it was a war zone.

At the very center of that perimeter was the dish atop of a large tower, casting a giant shadow over the rest of the complex. Directly north of it was a smaller tower with a large radio antenna. With the terrain, it was their only way of keeping contact with the colony.

There were five modules within the perimeter, and one old-fashioned garage. The modules were all dome-shaped, the two largest ones on the north side, housing the laboratory and command post. On the west wall were two adjoined modules serving as the barracks and mess hall. A second, smaller lab module was on the south wall, less than fifty feet from the southeast corner, where the garage was located. The latter was small, only housing two all-terrain cruisers, fuel drums, and some maintenance equipment.

Everyone was watching the thin grey cloud on the southeast wall. At first, they thought it was vapor from some sort of heating source. In a sense, they were correct, except that heat source was coming from *outside* the walls.

At its base was a heap of wreckage. Black deflated pieces of rubber stuck out from a crunched mound of charred metal and plastic. One of the vehicles had wrecked. Not just wrecked, but obliterated. Its fuel cell had caught fire. Given the fact that it was still warming the air around it, it was probably blazing until recently, extinguished by the heavy snowfall.

There was nobody on the watch posts. Nobody answered the radio.

"Ooookay," Angelo said. "Was not expecting this."

"Neither was I," Skerrit said under his breath.

They approached the east clearing where the flight deck was located. The snow was thick, making it difficult to see if there was any other damage to the complex.

"What should I do?" Angelo asked.

"Go ahead and set her down," Skerrit said. "Have the loading droids start moving the supplies. One way or another, this station is not going to be left unmanned unless absolutely necessary."

Angelo sighed and lowered the gunship to the deck. "As you wish."

Skerrit looked to the squad. "As for you guys, break out the weapons and prep for incursion. Not sure what's going on here, but until we know more, we're going in there as though we're retaking it from an enemy force."

"Aye, aye, sir!" the team replied in unison.

The gunship touched down, its pilot warily watching the vicinity to make sure some sort of combatant wasn't about to open fire on him. His hand remained on the joystick, ready to pull up at a drastic pace if necessary.

So far, nothing.

"Lowering ramp."

With a press of a button on his panel, the main entrance of the ship came down.

Naray and his fellow soldiers, armed with their standard W-12 blaster rifles, rushed onto the flight pad as though storming a beach. Naray moved north and found a firing position aligned with the northeast corner, his rifle pointed right at the main entrance. Pedro and Dodger took positions a few meters away from him, each watching the walls for movement.

Skerrit crouched near the gunship's port rotor and scanned the side of the perimeter with his binocs.

Nothing.

He gave a hand signal to Naray, who promptly led his team to the main entrance. Skerrit, Badejo, and Waterstan remained fifteen meters back, ready to provide cover fire.

Naray arrived at the gate. It was a sliding door, operated by gears which moved it on a rail. During their arrival, they thought it was shut. Only now did Naray realize it was actually shifted inwards.

Not only that, but its end was heavily malformed. It was bent in many places, its upper corner folded inward entirely. The rail was also heavily damaged, broken off from the north frame.

There was no point in running a bypass. This door wasn't keeping anybody out.

He waved to Skerrit's team to move on up.

"Jeez," the lieutenant muttered after getting a proper look at the gate.

"No blaster scoring. No burns at all," Naray said. "Almost looks like someone shot literal cannon balls at the thing."

Skerrit nodded in agreement, then readied himself to infiltrate. "Proceed inside."

Pedro went in first. He moved to the left and made way for Naray and Dodger. They panned their weapons in all directions, fingers resting on the trigger guards.

The only movement came from snow.

And a swinging piece of metal from one of the watch post stairwells.

It was the one for the center east watch post, located to their right. It had been broken apart by the base, the tower of steps collapsed in on itself, only to be held up by a few bolts on the top of the wall.

The metal support pillars were bent near the ground, one of them having snapped entirely.

Naray moved around the pile of wreckage, then sprinted to the side of a soldier wearing the same type of Nile-class battle suit he wore. Before he could state “Get the medic”, he realized the guy was way beyond dead. He had been brutalized, his spine broken in at least three places, causing his body to have an unnaturally flexible pose. One of his legs was missing and his gun was broken in half like a toothpick.

The others saw it too.

Now, it was certain: they were dealing with some sort of hostile force. The question was what. It did not stand to reason to believe this was a ‘who’. No human force in the galaxy would attack a military installation, not even one as outdated as Outpost Four, with nothing but brute force. Even if some sort of construction equipment was used for this incursion, it would have left some sort of residue. Oil, track marks, chips of paint on the gate and frame.

But there was nothing but aftermath.

Naray turned south towards the garage. From where he stood, he could see some minor damage to the structure.

"I'll check out the garage, generator, and south lab," he said to Skerrit.

The lieutenant nodded his approval. "My team will check the north side."

Both teams went their separate ways.

Naray's team moved in on the garage first. Pedro provided cover while the sergeant and corporal checked the entrance. The main door was open and seemingly operational. There was some chipping to the edge of the sliding door as well as a strange indentation on the wall. Looking at it, Naray could not help but picture some sort of colossal supervillain punching a crater with his fist into a building. Like the gate and stairwell, there was nothing to indicate weapons or even heavy equipment.

Unwilling to move on until finding some sort of clue, he rubbed his fingers into the crater, finding rigid metal slivers, plenty of snow, and a white strand of soft material. Initially, he had mistaken it for snow, as it shared the same color. Only when he pulled it from the crater did his mind make the connection to what it resembled.

"Hair?" Dodger asked.

"I… guess so," Naray said. He double-checked the garage. "Clear. Move on to the lab."

They moved fifty feet west and located the south lab module. Its east side was folded inward, the crushing of metal causing several see-through cracks in the structure, exposing the interior.

Its front entrance was working. Naray entered the building and found all sorts of geological lab equipment on the floor. The building had been hit hard enough to send every item that was not bolted down across the floor.

This time, there was some carbon scoring from a blaster rifle—on the *inside* of the building. The marks were near the big cracks at the point of impact, as though whoever was inside the lab was trying to shoot through them at the attacker.

Pedro stepped inside.

"Whoa! No bodies?"

"Negative," Naray said. "Where's Dodger?"

"He took the liberty of checking the generator," Pedro answered.

Naray gave one more look to the interior of the lab. There was nothing more to be done here. He knew the science staff were not present for the incident, as they were off site for an expedition.

The question now was where the hell was the rest of Alpha Team?

He and Pedro moved to the generator unit. It was an outside machine, roughly the size of a grocery check-out counter, wired to two cylinder-shaped towers. Basically, it was a mini nuclear reactor.

Naray checked the gauges. "Thank God."

His teammates knew what he was getting at.

Water was flowing in and out of the pipes, much to his relief. Even in this temperature, an overheated reactor would mean hell. And these reactors did not melt down like the ones of the pre-interstellar travel days. These smaller ones exploded after overheating. Even worse, they did not take multiple hours to several days to reach that critical point like the old reactors did. These reactors were great as long as they were cooled by a steady flow of water. But should that supply be cut off, it would take maybe forty-five minutes at most for the worst to occur unless the reactor was disabled from the Command Post.

"Team Two to Team One?"

"Go ahead, Sergeant," Skerrit replied through the radio.

"Power station's secure and operational without damage. Garage and South Lab have suffered damage, but can be repaired to an extent. Lab's got it the worst down here. We're now moving along the west perimeter wall. No further damage, so far."

"Any bodies?"

"Negative."

"Copy that. The sections up here are deserted. Radio controls are functional, but the tower has taken a bit of damage. Partly explains why there's been no transmission. That, and the fact nobody's here."

"Right. We'll check the dish on our way over to you."

"Copy. Meet us in the Command Post and we'll come up with a gameplan. Angelo, go ahead and bring the stuff inside. How's your ship's radio?"

"My ship's radio is fine," Angelo said. *"Unfortunately, at this distance... more specifically, in this location and in these weather*

conditions, I might have a hard time reaching the colony."

"Figures. Alright, let's get the supplies inside. And bring a body bag."

Naray shared a glance with his fellow soldiers.

"On the bright side, this got us off Pedro's case about the baby situation," he said.

They continued northwards to the Command Post. Finding tasks for the men on this first day was the least of Naray's worries now.

CHAPTER 6

Sleeping Ridge was a fascinating natural formation. According to theories by Toby Anderson and other scientists on-world, the rock had originally formed nearly a mile under the planet's surface, only to be lifted up by volcanic and seismic activity over the course of millions of years. The ridge extended for over a half mile, its lowest point on its western side. As the science team traveled eastwards, the ridge steadily rose like a stone ramp. Soon, the forms became more jagged and bizarre as they neared the largest section a few hundred yards past the ridge's center. The height of the rock dropped drastically, its top forming a sort of canopy overlooking several meters of open space.

Contrary to Toby's suggestion that the trees would reduce the accumulation of snow on the ground, the trip turned out to be slow and tedious. The windows were fogged over, the heat barely adequate to keep the passengers from shivering. Their gear rattled in the rear storage compartment, and the wiper blades and antifreeze worked tirelessly to keep the windshield clear.

Sasha was in the front passenger seat. She still had her gloves and scarf on. The heat was maxed out, yet it barely seemed to be anything more than lukewarm.

For centuries, humankind had developed land vehicles, and to this day, the basic problems persisted. She was aware that security rotation should have taken place by now. Hopefully, one of the new guys was a trained mechanic who could properly tend to the equipment.

The passengers were silent. Since departing from the crocodilian corpse, the only words spoken were from Toby. As to be expected from him, they were all about plans for future trips to the cavern and documents he wanted to get typed before alerting Crown Station of his findings.

Hardly anyone listened. All they could think about was getting to the warmth of Outpost Four in one piece. Something killed that saurian creature, and it could be anywhere. Something that big and strong would make short work of this cruiser and everyone in it. With that in mind, Toby's self-centered monologues went in one ear and out the other, as everyone's attention was focused on the outside.

Knowing something was out there made the foggy windows all the more frustrating—again, to everyone but Toby.

"...and after we get the thermal cutters, we can get some drones for initial entrance into the cavern. I know the military guys have some at the colony. I just need to think of a good reason to give to them."

Sasha couldn't take it anymore.

"I'm sure you'll think of something, Professor." She put her hands to the heater again. "Gosh, this is almost unbearable."

Toby made a jeering face. "You want to be a researcher? You need to get used to field conditions."

"Field conditions are one thing," she said. "Being given crappy supplies, all while bragging about no expense being spared, tends to be aggravating and demoralizing." She looked out the window. "Maybe we should get those drones you mentioned to do a sweep of the area and get a visual on what's out there."

Toby shook his head. "As far as they're concerned, there's nothing out here but us. Those drones are typically used for security purposes."

"Yeah? And?"

"I can't give the impression of a safety issue. Otherwise, they'll send several more staff up here. And if I tell them precisely what the problem is, a bunch of other scientists will demand to be flown to this location. No way am I allowing that until we have everything documented."

"Oh, gee," Beth groaned. "Good to know you've got your priorities straight."

Toby turned his head to look at her, his foot still on the accelerator. "Watch your tone. With just one phone call, I can have you working in less desirable locations than this. With even worse equipment."

"Um, sir?" George said, pointing forward. "Mind keeping your eyes on the road."

"There is no road," Toby quipped.

"Kind of reinforces my point," an even more nervous George said. "I'd like to not crash into anything. Today of all days."

Toby shook his head and faced forward. "Bunch of weak-minded sissies I'm forced to work with. I've traveled this area for two years. I know it like the back of my hand. Never once have I had an incident. Not even a bad bump."

THUMP!

The cruiser jolted, the left side briefly dragging after making contact with something.

Toby put his foot on the brake pedal, baring his teeth as the vehicle nearly spiraled into the side of a tree. It came to a stop less than a meter from collision, and only thanks to the snow that had bunched up on the right of the vehicle.

Not giving his staff an opportunity to make a retort of his recent statement, Toby put the vehicle in park and stepped outside. He looked at the trail from the point of impact. In the semi-circular skid mark, a lump protruded from the snow.

"What the hell did I hit?"

George was next to step out. "Oh, damn. I see red snow. I think that's blood. Probably an animal of some sort."

Immediately, Toby was filled with a new dose of energy. Even through the scarf and heavy snowfall, Sasha could make out the look on his face. The professor was thinking he had made another biological discovery.

Right away, he made a move towards the thing.

In unison, Sasha, George, and Beth sighed and followed him. As they reached the mass, they took in a pungent odor and the sight of meshed fur.

Without exercising an ounce of caution, Toby knelt by the thing and brushed the snow off of it.

"Good Lord!"

The others kept their distance, equally deterred by the smell and appearance of the thing. It was almost the size of a miniature horse, though with much shorter legs, thick black fur, and a long tail that looked like a giant nightcrawler. Long teeth extended from the ends of its pointed snout. Its small feet were double-jointed and equipped with thin claws, sharp as razor blades.

"Is that a rat?" Beth asked in disgust.

Toby nodded in delight.

George cupped a hand over his mouth. "A *big freaking* rat."

Toby continued brushing away the snow until the entire animal was revealed. It was five feet in body length; its tail adding an extra six. Judging from its heavy bulk, it weighed close to two-hundred pounds.

Blood pooled from its mouth and ears. Toby put his fingers to its skull and gently pushed in.

"Ick. Hit the guy in the head. Lights out in an instant."

It was a relief for the rest of the team.

"Good. Let's get out of here," Beth said. "I'm here to study ice. Not killer rodents. This isn't my specialty."

"Your specialty is whatever I say it is," Toby barked. "Now get over here and help me get a tarp on this thing."

Beth looked as though she would vomit as she moved to the cruiser's storage compartment.

"Wait," Sasha said. "You plan on bringing this thing along?"

"Why not?" Toby said. "We can fit it."

She could sense another endless spiel about documents and cataloging. The guy had discovered another unknown species. He wasn't thinking about the science; he was envisioning his name on a university building and whatever prize he may receive.

Beth brought a tarp over to him. She stopped a few steps shy of the creature. It may have been dead, but that didn't make it any less disgusting.

The professor scowled at her. "Come on. Not like it's going to bite you." He laughed at his own joke.

Beth inched closer, then tossed him one end of the tarp. He began wrapping it around the head of the creature.

"Tuck your side under its rear end," he instructed her. Beth had her hands close to her chest, looking at the rat as though it would resurrect and come at her with those horrible jaws. Toby bobbed his head, getting increasingly impatient. "Come on! Come on!"

Beth finally knelt down. Whimpering in disgust, she tried to get the edge of the tarp under the creature's hip.

The rat shook violently, the professor calling out in horror.

"AHHH!"

Beth squealed and jumped back, hands cupping her face. "Oh, Jesus! Oh, God!"

Toby lowered the animal's head and shook with laughter.

Sasha's look of disapproval went unseen by him. Even if it hadn't, the professor would not have cared.

George sniggered a bit. Unlike Toby, he did notice Sasha's look.

"What?" He shrugged. "It was a little funny."

"You are all assholes!" Beth said.

"Oh, have a sense of humor," Toby said. "Come on back. Let's get this thing wrapped up for real this time. George, come and help. This bad boy is heavy."

The glaciologist shrunk a few inches. "Alright." He sounded like a kid given a chore by his parents. Sasha didn't begrudge him that; she would've sounded precisely the same way.

Beth took a step to return, only to jump to the side in fright.

"Now what?" Toby said.

Beth's eyes were on a lump in the snow. "There's something over here. I see more blood." She leaned forward, then stepped back further, eyes wide. "There's something else dead over here!"

"Another rat?" Toby said in excitement.

"I… I don't know!"

Toby secured the tarp to keep it from blowing away, then hurried to the thing. Sasha joined him, concerned about the way Beth was acting. This wasn't the typical fear one expressed when looking at a large rodent. This was something else entirely.

She and Toby arrived at the thing and brushed the dusting of snow off the black exterior. At once, they jumped away.

"Jesus!" Toby said, his excitement gone entirely.

Sasha put her hands to her cheeks. This was not a rat. It wasn't an animal at all. It was a human corpse dressed in military gear. The face was gone entirely, likely snacked on by the rat. The rest of the body had suffered completely different injuries. One of the legs had been torn off entirely, and the abdomen had been crunched in as though a pile driver had slammed down on it, causing the chest to become inflated.

"That's one of our guys," Toby said in a gasp.

Sasha composed herself and knelt down to check the tag on the right shoulder. She read the name and stood up.

"This was Charley Yuel." She spun on her feet and scanned their surroundings. "What was he doing all the way out here? I don't see their vehicle."

Toby picked up the soldier's damaged rifle. It had been cracked in half like a toothpick.

"I don't think the rat did this to him," he said. "I think it found his corpse recently." He watched Sasha inspect Charley's radio. It had been smashed during his fatal moments. "You're wasting your time. For once, I'm agreeing with your original assessment. Whatever killed the reptile probably did this. With that in mind, we want to make our way to the outpost. First, let's get the specimen loaded up, and we'll get out of here."

"What about Charley?" George asked.

"Not enough room for him," Toby said.

"Wait… you mean to suggest we should just leave him here to be snacked on by other rats?" Sasha said.

"I doubt it'll make a difference to Charley," Toby said without a single hint of compassion. "Besides, the new security team would rather handle it anyway."

Sasha inhaled deeply, stopping herself from slapping the guy across the face. It was a temptation that would have failed had it not been for the next unexpected event.

BANG! BANG! BANG!

All eyes turned northwest. Those were undeniably blaster shots.

"That's coming from the ridge," Sasha said.

More shots rang out. This time, they caught glimpses of the red flashes from blaster bolts streaming from underneath the crest of Sleeping Ridge.

"There!" George shouted.

He led the charge, though only for about five steps before nearly tripping in the deep snow.

Sasha helped him up and ran alongside him. Somebody was out there and was in trouble. There was no thought to what they would do once they got there.

"Wait!" Toby called after them. His graduate students ignored him. Standing near the dead rat, the geologist stood unsure what to do, his scarf threatening to fly away in the wind. "What about the vehicle?!"

This time, Sasha answered. "It gets steep up here."

In normal circumstances, that would not be a problem for the cruiser, but with all this snow, they would just spin tires.

With that in mind, Toby decided to just stand by and wait. Sasha knew his mindset. The group had individual short-range communicators. If something went wrong, he would know. Besides, if they were getting attacked, odds are he would hear their screams and abandon them in favor of saving his own ass.

Sasha chose to focus on what was ahead of her.

Another blaster bolt streaked from under the crest. A grotesque sound, a mixture of hellish hatred and agonizing pain, roared out from where it struck. The burst of sparks created enough of a flash which outlined the cone-shaped snout and rounded body of a second killer rodent.

Sasha slowed. The beast was at least as large as the one they had hit with the cruiser. The way it fell on its side indicated it quickly succumbed to the burning hot projectile. Still, going anywhere near the thing was not exactly something she was eager to do.

George got a few steps ahead of her and began waving his arms. "Hello! This is Dr. George Morty! I'm here with Dr. Toby Anderson's research team. Please, do not shoot! We're coming towards you."

"Hurry up!" the guy in the ridge called back. "There might be others!"

Sasha knew that voice. There was a husky quality to it, made worse by long exposure to the cold.

As she and her colleagues reached the ridge, her instinct proved correct.

Sitting up in that ridge was Corporal Roland Welker. Generally, he was a no-nonsense type of guy, except when he was with his buddies, then he was full of jokes that were nothing more than sexual innuendos. Right now, he was definitely the former version of himself. And the reason was obvious.

The red snow by his leg indicated he had lost quite a bit of blood while he was holed up in the cave. He leaned against the inner wall of the cave, rifle pointed outward, tilted upward slightly as the friendlies approached.

He was tired, his lips chapped, his battle suit coated in ice and frozen snow.

Sasha moved down by his leg. “Oh, gosh, Corporal. What are you doing out here?”

Welker took a breath. “We had to evacuate. It burst through the gate. Started wrecking the outpost from within. There was nowhere we could hide. We ran north and tried to set up a trap, but it caught up with us.”

Sasha looked through the tear in his pants. His leg was badly lacerated, but he had stapled it shut and slowed the bleeding.

She clicked the transmitter on her comm. “Dr. Anderson?”

“Everything alright over there?”

"No. We've got Roland Welker over here. He's hurt pretty bad."

"We can stuff him into the cruiser, if he can hobble over here."

"We might need something faster," she said. "Please use the cruiser's radio to call the outpost. The new guys should be in by now, and if so, that gunship ought to still be on site. See if you can reach anybody. If you do, tell them to fly out here right away, and to have a harness prepped."

"Alright."

Sasha gave a quiet thanks to whatever high power existed that the professor did not give her a hard time on the matter. He was probably still working on loading up the rat thing anyway. Regardless, help should be here soon.

Her mind went back to Welker's explanation. It dawned on her that he could not possibly have been talking about the rats. \

Wrecking the outpost? What could he mean by that? Those rodents were big, but not THAT big.

"Wait…" she said to him. "You said 'it' started wrecking the outpost. What's 'it'?"

Welker grimaced in pain. Had he not been so lightheaded, he would have spoken more clearly on the matter. As of now, he was fighting to stay awake.

"The beast. The white beast."

"What kind of beast?" Beth asked, almost afraid to know the answer.

Welker had a rise in energy. His eyes narrowed and his face wrinkled with sheer hatred as he stared into the woods. He was not only a sole survivor; he was a man with a score to settle.

"A Yeti."

CHAPTER 7

"Move it, gentlemen! Move it! Move it! Move it!" Naray barked. The marines were quick to move through the command post to the exit. The building was not complicated. It was comprised of a communication's center and operations room—both adjacent to one another—had an office with two desks for the commanding officers on duty, an armory, and a kitchen area.

The unit was in the middle of assessing the damage and coming up with a plan to repair the radio tower when Angelo radioed from the gunship. He had received a call from the science team. Apparently, they had found one of Alpha Team's members.

Naray led the troops to the main gate, keeping his voice loud to motivate his teammates.

"Today, ladies! Today!"

They filed into the gunship, Naray and Skerrit last to step aboard. As soon as the door slammed shut, the aircraft lifted off and sped north. In a few short moments, they were flying over trees straight towards the big mountain.

"Hell of a first day here," Pedro remarked.

"No shit," Badejo said. "Not even fifteen minutes into outpost duty, and we're already busy as hell. We've barely been able to poke fun at you about baby-making."

"If I have my way, you'll have plenty of time later," Skerrit said.

Naray knew the tone. Skerrit was an honorable soldier, always doing everything that was required of him. But he was not stupid or heartless, and he was not the type to put his men in unnecessary risk.

"You're planning a return trip, aren't you, sir?"

Skerrit nodded. "Whatever was out there, it drove an entire squad of armed soldiers out from the safest place in the region. And now the place is even less secure. We've only got a couple of working turrets. Radio antenna is down. And we don't even know what we're dealing with. As far as I'm concerned, staying here is a death sentence. We're going back. When we return, it'll be with a properly equipped task force."

It was news the men were glad to hear.

"Good!" Dodger said. "That means I won't have to wait as long to see the look on what's-her-name's face when she inevitably sees Pedro on another date. Who knows? Maybe he'll have two different babies from two different mammas arriving around the same time."

"No, freaking way," Pedro said. "You're just jealous because you haven't gotten any in six months. We should change your name from Dodger to 'Dodged', since every woman on-world avoids you like the plague."

The team laughed at that, including Dodger.

"Way to turn it around on me," he said.

Naray kept his eyes to the window. According to Angelo, the friendlies were located on a rock structure on the mountainside called Sleeping Ridge.

After two miles, the landscape began to elevate.

"I think I see the rock structure they were talking about," Angelo said.

"Tell them to fire up a flare," Naray said.

Angelo relayed the message to the friendlies. Half a minute later, a ball of flame rose over the trees.

"I see it!"

He decreased altitude until he was a few meters over the treetops, continuing with haste until he was near the strange rock structure.

The trees were spaced out enough near the huge granite ridge to allow visibility of the personnel below.

"There they are." Naray opened the side door. "Hold here, Angelo."

"Nah, I thought I'd visit the North Pole," the pilot retorted.

Naray put a harness over himself and prepped a harness for the injured soldier. Lieutenant Skerrit joined him at the door and put a hand on his shoulder to make sure he had the sergeant's full attention.

"We don't have a lot of time. Tell all of them we're evacuating. As commander of our post, I am ordering those scientists into this ship. Their science project can wait until we get a handle on the situation."

"Got it, Lieutenant."

Naray put himself over the side of the vessel and roped thirty feet to the forest floor. He landed on a rocky slope covered in snow and was immediately greeted by a man and a woman in thick winter clothing. They helped steady him and offered to help get the harness on the fallen man.

The soldier was seated upright against the rock wall. Next to him was a female scientist with strands of black hair coming out of her hood. The layers of clothing covering her body almost appeared to weigh more than her. Though young and petite, she acted with the professionalism and promptness of some military officers.

"Thank God you're here," she said to Naray. "He's lost blood. He needs to be in a proper medical facility."

Naray approached them. "Are there any others?"

The injured soldier shook his head. "They're all dead. I'm all that's left."

Naray took him at his word. After what he saw at the outpost, it did not seem far-fetched at all to think Alpha Team was annihilated.

The soldier, Roland Welker, was someone he had seen in passing. Naray had never worked directly with the guy. Looking at the dead rats with fresh burn wounds from blaster bolts, he knew the corporal was not someone to be trifled with. He was a crack shot even in this borderline delirious state.

Then came the realization of giant rats in the area.

The female scientist with black hair noticed how he was glancing back at the corpses. "Yeah, it appears an entire ecosystem has been unleased onto the mountainside."

"Got it," Naray said. "You can explain on the way back. I'm Sergeant Naray of Bravo Team."

The three scientists identified themselves.

"Sasha Serigami."

"Dr. George Morty."

"Beth Kruse."

"Good to meet y'all," Naray said. "Listen up. The outpost has undergone an attack. There's been extensive damage inside the perimeter. The gate is trashed."

The three scientists gasped in unison.

"What about the power core?" Sasha asked.

"Stable," Naray assured her. "But the station's antenna is down. We don't have long-range communications, and there's no guarantee we can repair it. To sum it up: we're truly alone out here. Besides, it takes almost eight hours for someone to fly out here to begin with. We're not chancing it. You are all ordered to board the gunship and fly home with us."

George quickly approached. "No arguments from me!"

"Same here," Beth said.

"Let's get Corporal Welker up there first," Sasha said.

She assisted Naray in getting the harness on the injured soldier.

"Watch out," Welker groaned. "More are coming."

"More…" Naray realized what he was talking about. He could hear the cackling of other rats in the woods. Their sounds almost resembled those of hyenas in the African safari, striking a sense of dread in their victims.

He took off his harness and extended it to Beth. "Let's move now." He secured the clips, then gave the signal to the guns looking down from the ship to start up the hoist.

Both Welker and Beth were lifted high into the bird. The soldiers up there got the harnesses off them and sent both lines back to ground level.

"Your turns," Naray said to Sasha and George, thrusting the harnesses into their hands. George wasted no time getting his on. Sasha, meanwhile, was looking even more panicky. She was looking past Naray into the woods.

"The professor!" She engaged her short-range comm. "Toby! You need to get over here! We're evacuating in the military gunship. The situation's worse than we thought."

After a short pause, the man's voice came through.

"Wait, we're abandoning the site?"

"For now," Sasha said. "You have to get over here now."

"I'm not leaving the specimens! There's too much at stake."

"Are you for real?!" Sasha groaned.

Naray took the device from her and spoke into it. "Listen, Doctor. As the lady said, we're evacuating. And by protocol, we are not permitted to leave any civilians behind. So, get your ass over here so we can take off."

"Just leave without me. I'll be fine. Don't bring any scientists when you return. There's stuff I need to get in order first."

Naray looked at Sasha.

She gave a deriding snigger and nodded her head. *Yeah, he's that pathetic.*

"You don't get to make such decisions, Professor." As he spoke, George was lifted into the gunship. Naray shook a finger at Sasha, informing her to finish clipping her harness. "I'll tell you one last time: make your way to our position so we can get out of here. If I have to beat your ass and drag you aboard, make no mistake, I'll damn well do it."

This time, the professor was going the method of radio silence.

Naray leaned his helmet mic to his lips. "Guys, lift Ms. Serigami. I've got one more, and he's refusing to tag along."

"I know the location," Sasha said. "I can direct them towards you so you don't have to hike all the way back here."

"Appreciate it," Naray said. He liked her already. "Where's he at? Other end of these fresh tracks you made?"

"Correct," Sasha replied.

"Got it."

Naray unslung his rifle and followed the trail with a sprint. Behind him, Sasha was hoisted from the ground into the gunship.

He was a hundred paces into the woods when he heard the gunship change direction. Sasha had informed the guys where to go.

The unnerving sounds from the distance increased. Naray swept his surroundings with the muzzle of his rifle, searching for any movement within that haze of near-horizontal snow.

From his right came an intense growl.

Naray stopped in his tracks and faced the threat.

"Good God."

Two rats as large as tigers approached them. Their stubby little legs were almost invisible between the snowfall and their fat bodies. In any other context, Naray would have found them comical. But not this time, as they had no trouble carrying the snarling beasts in his direction. Their intent was plain on their faces.

Fabric and blood strands dangled from their teeth. Behind them, a flayed human corpse lay unburied in the snow. It was a soldier from Alpha Team, whose corpse became an easy meal for the rodents. Easy did not mean better. His flesh was probably hard and chewy. Naray's, on the other hand, was fresh and warm.

He hit the beasts with a steady stream of blaster bolts. The flaming hot rounds cut through fur and flesh with ease, erasing the rats' intimidating disposition. Now, the warm meat was theirs, as they lay in the ground, taking in the smell of their own sizzling flesh as they succumbed to their wounds.

Naray pressed on.

He barely made three steps before a new sound reached his ears. This was not cackling rats, nor was it sounds of animalistic aggression. This was mechanical. An engine.

Headlights beamed on ahead of him. An engine roared.

That son of a bitch Toby Anderson was trying to drive off.

Naray's temper was almost as hot as the ammo in his gun. He pointed his gun in the direction of the vehicle's silhouette and squeezed the trigger, deliberately firing high enough to miss, but keeping the bolts low enough to be seen.

The message was received.

Toby swerved to the left, sideswiping a tree. He stormed out of the driver's seat and stomped towards the sergeant as he approached the cruiser. Toby Anderson was exactly how Naray pictured: tall, sporting fogged-up glasses, and absolutely full of himself.

"What is the matter with you?" the professor yelled. "You're a maniac! I'm gonna have you court martialed for aggravated assault with a deadly weapon, and then—OOF!"

A blow to his gut dropped the idiot to his knees and shut him up.

It was satisfying for Naray. He hated this guy already. He could only imagine Sasha's misery of having to work with him long-term.

Naray grabbed the professor by the jacket and lifted him up. "You're leaving with us, even if I have to break all four of your limbs to do it."

For once, Toby got the idea.

The gunship arrived overhead. Angelo positioned it just above the treetops. The side door was still open, and from it descended two ropes with harnesses at their end.

Naray was in the middle of reaching for one of those ropes when something else caught his eye. It was fast and large, moving at a similar altitude as the aircraft. His imagination almost mistook the item as a meteor in the way it moved in a downward trajectory… except when he first saw it, it was moving upward. Like a tennis ball chucked high in the air, only to eventually angle downward.

This object was no tennis ball. It was maybe ten feet in width, shaped more like a slab than a ball, and clearly rigid.

A rock.

"Guys! You've got incoming!"

The rock struck the gunship's port rotor. Panicked screams and shouts of "HOLY SHIT!" were nearly lost behind the intense groan of straining mechanics and crunching canopy. Bits of metal and wood rained down around Naray and Toby, both men covering their heads while the gunship spiraled out of control.

Angelo's transmissions became garbled, but Naray could sense the guy fighting to stay calm. The words "Shut up back there!" made it through his receiver.

"He's gonna crash!" Toby shouted.

Naray watched the vessel spin southwards across the canopy, leaving a trail of broken tree limbs in its wake.

"The pilot is trying to set it down as gently as he can," he said.

The ship continued its downward trajectory.

"Brace yourselves!"

Two seconds later—*CRASH!*

A thunderous echo from the impact raced deep into the mountainside.

Naray's heart jumped into his throat. "Bravo Team! Lieutenant?" He got no response through the radio. If anything was working in his favor, it was the fact he had a clear trail to the crash site. "Come on, Professor. We need your cruiser."

Toby's face went white as the snow. "Are you mad, Sergeant? Did you see what just happened? That wasn't a pebble. Something threw a boulder at your buddies. Something *big!* You know as well as I do, your buddies are dead. Our best bet is to make a run back to the outpost."

Naray would've kneed the jerk in the nuts had the situation not been so dire. Instead, he settled with shoving his rifle muzzle in his gut.

"Get in the damn driver's seat."

That seemed to work. Toby went into the vehicle without a fuss. Naray had a good read on the guy. He had seen many assholes like him, both on this world and on others. He was a guy who relied on his so-called status to talk a big game, but when faced with meaningful opposition, he fell apart easily.

Naray took the front passenger seat and watched for any adversaries while the professor drove them to the crash. The cruiser bumped over all sorts of debris and zigzagged to get around the larger branches.

"You've made a grave mistake, pointing that thing at me," Toby growled.

Naray could not believe this guy.

"Dude, just shut up with the tough talk. I could literally shoot you right here and now, and nobody would even know. By the time they found your corpse, the rats would have stripped you clean."

Toby gulped at that realization. He wasn't sure if Naray was serious or not, but wisely chose not to risk it. Naray wasn't even sure if he was serious or not. It all depended on how much more trouble the doctor would be in the coming hours.

One thing was certain: they weren't flying back to home base anymore. Now, all they could hope for was to fortify the outpost and fix that damn antenna.

They saw smoke up ahead.

"There it is," Naray said.

The gunship was on its portside. Both rudders had broken away completely. The center of the aircraft was cracked wide open. An odor of leaked fuel permeated the air. Sparks spat from the exposed engine, causing great tension for the two men inside the cruiser. Angelo managed to skid the bird between some trees and avoid a full-on crash landing, which would have resulted in a heavy explosion, but only just barely so.

The boarding ramp swung like a door, scraping snow and frozen soil. From the stern of the gunship came a dazed Pedro. Badejo was right behind him, physically pushing him forward.

"The hell was that?" Pedro shouted, forgetting that the guy was only a few inches away.

"How do you expect me to know?" Badejo replied.

Dodger and Waterstan stepped out. The medic was bleeding from his hairline, but appeared to be alright. He stopped by the door and waved for the three civilian workers to come out.

Sasha had Beth's arm around her shoulder. George and Lieutenant Skerrit were helping Corporal Welker step outside. The sole survivor of Alpha Team hobbled on his one good leg, appearing much more alert than when they found him in the cave.

Toby brought the cruiser as close to them as he could. Naray opened his door and stepped out to help get Welker into the backseat.

"It's gonna be cramped, but unless you'd rather head back on foot..." he said.

"No complaints here," Waterstan said.

The troops allowed Sasha and Beth into the vehicle first. Next was Skerrit, George, and Welker. The lieutenant ushered the two men inside, then ordered Pedro and Badejo into the rear row of seats.

"We all dread outpost duty," Badejo said. "If you ask me, I'd *kill* for a standard, boring day of playing with a deck of cards."

"Let's get out of here alive, and you can play with yourself later," Skerrit remarked. He turned his eyes to the downed gunship. "Angelo? Where the hell are ya?"

"Is he hurt?" Naray asked.

"No," Skerrit said, squinting in confusion. "He was just there. He wanted to seal a fuel leak under the forward compartment to prevent an explosion, then he was going to join us over here."

The two men watched. Angelo was not there.

"AGH!"

The gunship rocked violently, rolling onto its back and exposing its underside. Behind the fog of vapor and fumes, a white humanoid shape emerged. Humanoid was the word, for it was shaped almost precisely like a human. But that was where the similarities ended. Its arms were longer in proportion to its body than a man. Then there was its height. It stood at least fifteen feet high. Maybe even seventeen or eighteen feet—and as the age-old expression goes: built like a brick shithouse. Its body was covered in thick fur as white as the snow… the same kind of fur Naray had found embedded in the garage wall.

It turned to face the cruiser and its occupants. A sharp exhale from its nostrils punched a brief hole in the vapor curtain separating it and the team. Its face was darker than the rest of its body, its snout protruding slightly from its thick gorilla-style skull. Lips peeled back, revealing rows of curved fangs that were clearly meant for ripping meat off the bone. Yellow eyes stared at the humans, all at once animalistic but conveying some degree of intelligence. And with intelligence came cruelty, demonstrated by its greeting to Bravo Team.

It held Angelo in its right hand, squeezing his hips and abdomen in a single grip. His left arm had been torn out by the roots, making way for a waterfall of blood to spill over the white fur on its wrist.

"What in God's name?" Skerrit muttered.

"What is that?" Waterstan shouted.

"You seriously have to ask?" Dodger said. "It's a damn YETI!"

Toby and Sasha shared a look of apprehension, equally terrified of the very sight of the unholy beast, while also having a moment of realization. Either they knew it was here, or they had stumbled upon their own clues.

Angelo was still alive, his scream now a prolonged groan.

The beast held his empty arm socket to eye level, amused by the bodily damage it had just inflicted. Seeing that its victim was still conscious, it took hold of his right leg. It looked at him, then at the people in and around the cruiser.

It barked a thunderous grunt.

"Put him down!" Waterstan shouted, rifle aimed at the thing's head.

The beast grunted again, then tore Angelo's leg off at the knee. The poor pilot squealed in considerable pain, his pitch doubling after the creature went on to tear off his other leg.

By now, all the troops except Welker were out of the vehicle. Even the injured corporal from Alpha Team had moved to the open door in order to point his rifle at the thing.

"Light him up!" Skerrit ordered.

A storm of blaster bolts, like blazing hot raindrops, streamed at the beast. Sparks flew off its fur coat, barely managing to even scorch the outer layer, let alone burn through the creature's flesh.

It stepped back in mild frustration, the shots inflicting minor pain, but nothing more than that. The only thing it appeared concerned about was its eyes. One hand was kept over its face, the other raising Angelo like a drumstick, then battering his skull on the hull of the gunship.

As the pilot's remains splattered over the aircraft and surrounding snow, the team of soldiers found themselves on the verge of breaking ranks.

Blaster bolts continued hitting the thing, but it did not appear fazed at all. Its hair proved not just adept to protect it from the frigid cold, but against all types of threats, whether it be the teeth of a rival beast, or the fires of hell itself.

Skerrit was quick to realize this standoff would not end well.

"Let's go! Move! Move!"

The men followed his instructions, squeezing into the seats.

"Pardon me, Ma'am," Dodger said as he practically crushed Sasha against the far side.

Waterstan opened the rear compartment, wincing in surprise after seeing the cargo inside. "What the—"

"Don't worry about what's in there. Just get in!" Skerrit said.

The beast began stepping around the wreckage, growling as though announcing its desire to give each and every one of them a similar punishment as Angelo.

Naray threw himself onto the roof of the cruiser. "Punch it, Professor!"

Toby shifted into reverse and gunned the accelerator. The cruiser backed several feet over its tracks, only to soon hit a mound of snow.

"Shit!" the driver exclaimed.

The beast growled again. This time, it almost sounded like a laugh.

Puny humans. You think you can get away so easily?

"Wow, Professor? Do all academics have the same idea of running away as you?" Dodger shouted.

"Sorry, I guess I forgot the protocol for outrunning a damn Yeti in eighteen inches of snow!" Toby shot back.

The tires spun, unable to gain traction.

Savoring the experience of watching its prey in a state of utter panic, the beast came around the bow of the gunship. It bared its teeth once more, presenting them a crooked smile straight from the pits of Hades.

Naray, still belly-down on the cruiser's roof, took aim at the creature's face. His finger rested on the trigger, ready to let loose a futile stream of energy bolts. His rational mind pestered him with the knowledge that his weapon was no deterrent to this beast; no more than shooting a pellet gun at a Tyrannosaurus Rex.

He inhaled, barely suppressing an overwhelming sense of terror that was determined to burst out of him in a deafening scream.

The smell of fuel filled his nose.

Naray lifted his head, the fear temporarily gone, the blood rush of a new idea sweeping it away. Down at the wreck, a puddle of fuel was melting the snow and soaking the ground.

Its fur may be able to withstand the heat of blaster bolts, but maybe a fireball of ignited Idorion fuel would be a different story.

Only one way to find out.

Naray pointed his muzzle at the ground near the creature's feet and unloaded the rest of his battery magazine. Hot sparks popped off with each impact, each one tiny and insignificant, until one of them touched the fuel.

An overcast of blazing orange blinded the group.

With a rumbling *BOOM,* the gunship and all of its contents ignited. In its place rose a sprouting flower made of hot fire and metal fragments.

The Yeti howled in an assertion of pain and fury. This time, its fur was insignificant in deflecting the heat. Coated with flames on its shoulders and back, the beast turned on its heel and retreated deep into the woods. Each step shook the ground like drumbeats, gradually getting quieter and more distant.

Naray slid himself off the cruiser and joined Waterstan in the storage compartment. They discarded the folded shelter, the rat corpse, and some other supplies, then banged on the wall to signal they were secure.

Toby put the vehicle in forward gear and tapped on the accelerator. The cruiser rocked forward and back, slowly finding traction.

He turned the cruiser south in the direction of Outpost Four.

Naray and Waterstan watched the forest, now lit by the glow of a raging fire. Slowly but truly, the snowstorm was getting the better of it, pelting the rain with thick flakes. That, combined with the clumps of snow falling from the canopy, would soon return the foot of the mountain to its usual frozen state.

"Go figure," the medic said. "No wonder nobody could find Sasquatch. Turns out he was on the other side of the freaking galaxy."

CHAPTER 8

The one good grace the team had so far today was the drive back to Outpost Four was uneventful and smooth. As soon as they reached the gate, Toby parked the cruiser alongside the wall and everyone made their way through the breach.

By then, dusk was falling.

There was no time to take a break. Bravo Team went straight to work fortifying the place. Waterstan tended to Roland Welker in the infirmary. Blood transfusions got the corporal back to his natural state. Proper bandaging and antibiotics were applied to his gash. What was most appreciated by the guy were the painkillers.

Naray knew the lieutenant would soon debrief the guy on what had occurred here, and wanted to be present to hear the details for himself. For the moment, the sergeant was at the front gate with George and Pedro. Blowtorches were applied to the thick metal door and large pieces of scrap metal. Despite the paralyzing cold, the men were sweating bullets. The glaciologist self-admittedly was not the handiest guy in the universe, or even the planet, but with some instruction, he was able to assist the two soldiers in their barricade.

The sergeant looked up at the watch post at the northeast corner. Dodger was at the gun, keeping watch for any Yetis, or whatever else was lurking out there. During the ride over, Sasha Serigami mentioned something that, frankly, sounded like a freaking dinosaur. Just the thought of such a thing was extra motivation for the men to work with haste.

Naray carefully ran his flame over a metal beam, gradually connecting it to the pillar. The door itself was already jammed tight, and there was no way of correcting its form with the available equipment. An entire maintenance team would have to be flown out here for any meaningful repairs to be done. That was an instance where Legacy truly would spare no expense. Once they were aware of a confirmed threat in the north region, they would probably replace all weaponry with something more top-of-the-line, and double the security staff, if not triple it. Maintenance staff and proper machinery would be on site at all times. Up until now, all that really mattered was the satellite dish, and the top brass did not consider anything on the planet to be of any threat.

No longer was that the case.

Sounds of heated tempers lifted Naray's attention from his welding. He lowered his goggles and looked to the south lab. Dr. Toby Anderson was kicking some sort of cannister after inspecting the inside of the wrecked module.

"I can't believe this. I absolutely cannot believe this!"

By his side was Sasha. Even in the dim evening light, her misery could be seen from a mile away.

Biting her lip, she slapped her hands on her legs and shook her head.

"You do realize a bunch of people are dead, Professor? There's bigger issues than the loss of your specimen and the lab. At least those things can be replaced. The lives of Alpha Team and that pilot cannot."

"This is the kind of thing those guys signed up for," Toby said in a tone so dismissive, one would think he was trying to illicit a response from the other men.

For a short while, Naray had felt a ping of guilt for going as far as to point a gun at the doc earlier. Threatening people in such a way was not something to be taken lightly. Now, he was impressed with himself for not squeezing the trigger.

Sasha clearly couldn't take much more of it herself. The two scientists went separate ways. Toby went to the main lab, while Sasha took a walk over to the gate.

"Looking for better company?" Naray asked.

The graduate student exhaled through her mouth. "Not sure what's worse; that asshole, or the big furry thing out there? At least we can say that's just an aggressive animal."

"What's his deal?" Pedro asked.

"He's all pissed that apparently you guys couldn't manage to squeeze into the storage compartment with the rat-thing," Sasha said. "Moreso, he's pissed that we discarded his imager. I guess we were supposed to wedge ourselves in with all of his equipment."

"Aw, poor guy," Naray said while making an exaggerated frown.

Sasha nodded in agreement with the sentiment. "Also, he's still bent out of shape that a bunch of people will inevitably be coming here if and when we fix that antenna. Even now, with our lives hanging in the balance, he's focused on getting sole credit for the new biological discoveries."

"He wants to be known as the guy who discovered 'Alien Sasquatch'," Pedro said with a chuckle.

"That about sums it up," Sasha replied. "That, and everything else that's shown up recently."

"Yeah, like that dinosaur thing we found," George said with a shudder.

"You said it was dead," Pedro said.

George looked over at him. "Yeah, but who's to say there isn't another one?"

Pedro thought about it, then got back to work on applying the barricade.

Sasha looked at the flimsy pieces of metal covering the gap in the entrance. "Do you think this'll be enough? I mean, look at what that thing did when it attacked Alpha Team."

"Nope," Naray said bluntly. Understanding her concern, he had Sasha peer through the gaps between the metal beams. "You see those little black things in the snow, just a few yards out?"

"Yep."

"Those are mines. Here, look…" He turned to a nearby case and pulled another mine out of it. "Don't worry, I disabled it."

"I appreciate that," Sasha jested.

She gave a look at the thing's thick disk shape. It resembled a large hockey puck, roughly fourteen inches in diameter. Its topside had slits where the thing opened up like a flower.

"I'm assuming these things are made to detonate when something trips their sensor."

"Bingo," Naray said. "See, the top part opens, and an explosive charge spirals up, almost like a firework spinner. It raises maybe six feet or so, and goes boom. Packs a hell of a punch, too."

Sasha understood.

"I see. Since we can't keep the thing out, we might as well bait the son of a bitch."

"You're a natural," Naray said. "Maybe you picked the wrong career."

Sasha managed to laugh at that. "Don't know if soldiering is my forte. Though, I wouldn't mind seeing that hairy bastard get blown to smithereens. How many of those mines you got?"

Naray frowned and pointed to the ones outside. "Those, and the one I showed you."

Sasha pointed at another puck-shaped device attached to the sergeant's vest. "Wait? What about those?"

He looked down and realized what she was getting at. "Oh, this? This is called a firestick. Probably not the best of names, but it's still a handy explosive. They're not as strong as the mines, but they're enough to ruin somebody's day."

"I see," Sasha said. "Usually the guys around here don't wear them."

"We're supposed to when on duty," Pedro said. "It's easy to get lazy in a place like this. They're basically the grenades of our time, though the firesticks are stronger."

Naray held his up and pointed to a breakable seal on one edge of the puck. "You break this, then press the button inside. That starts the fuse. When you do that, a handle comes out the opposite end. You have about ten seconds to throw it. So easy, a monkey could figure it out."

"That it is," she replied.

Naray turned to look at the antenna tower. Skerrit had been working with Badejo on repairing it since they arrived. Now, the lieutenant was walking to the Command Post. Naray knew what was up: he had gotten word that Welker was in good enough condition for a debriefing.

"Keep working, you guys," he said to Pedro and George.

Sasha joined him on the way up to the Command Post. "Is there anything I can do to help?"

"Not at the moment," the sergeant said. "Just stay alive. And try not to stress out. I know that's asking a lot, but still…"

"I'll do my best," she said.

They followed Skerrit into the Command Post. There, they found Roland Welker on his feet inside the communications control center. He had a beer in hand and a bitter look on his face.

"Lieutenant. Sergeant," he said in acknowledgement of the higher ranks entering the building. They shivered briefly and adjusted to the warmth of the building.

"Corporal," Skerrit replied. "Glad to see you up and about."

"Your medic did fine work." Welker tilted his head at Waterstan, who gave a thumbs up from the infirmary at the west end of the module. He was busy sorting through his medical supplies. Given the circumstances, he clearly wanted to have an inventory of everything they had.

"Good to hear," Skerrit said. "So, what happened? I mean, we got the gist—Yeti came in, smashed stuff up, blah-blah."

"So much happened so fast," Welker said. "Luckily, the researchers were off-site. We were conducting normal operations. Two of our guys thought they heard a tree fall, and decided to go and check it out. We thought it was weird, since there was no heavy wind at the time, and let's be real—they had nothing better to do."

Naray put the pieces together. "They found the tree *and* what dropped it."

"Precisely," Welker said. "They alerted us on the radio and we got geared up. It killed one of them on the spot. The other retreated to the outpost in the cruiser. Unfortunately, the damn door is so slow to open, so he wasn't able to just speed right on in. He pulled up by the wall, and the thing closed in on him. He got out right as the thing smashed the vehicle. Didn't do him much good though. By then, the door was open, and the thing chased him inside the perimeter. That's when it smashed the stairwell to the watch post."

"Damn," Naray whispered, his mind creating a movie based on the corporal's narrative.

"We hit it with everything we had, but it kept coming. And we didn't want to use explosives inside the perimeter. Not with the reactor. On top of that, we quickly came to realize hiding in the compound would only delay the inevitable. The thing can tear through these modules as though they're made of Lego. So, one of the guys distracted it by the south lab while the rest of us went out the gate. The idea was to trap the thing inside and buy us time to set up a proper trap for it. Unfortunately, the private—Rodgers was his name—didn't make it. Even worse, our plan didn't work out as well as we thought. Again, the door is so old, it opens and closes at a snail's pace. Normally, that's of no consequence, but when you have a damn albino *King Kong* coming at you—" He shrugged, figuring the guys understood. "Anyway, it caught the door before it could shut entirely. And, holy shit, it literally bent the thing out of shape and managed to squeeze itself through the opening. All we could do was run. And run, we did. Managed to get all the way to the ridge. By then, it had tracked us all down and tore us to shreds. Almost got me too. The thing has some nasty nails on its fingertips. I literally dodged getting snatched up by a millimeter. Unfortunately, its nail caught my leg. It got distracted with one of the other guys, allowing me to crawl to the cavern under the ridge and hole up. And that's where I stayed until you all showed up."

Skerrit whistled. "You never saw anything bizarre before then?"

Welker shook his head. "Nothing. Then the earthquake happened and the big cavern opened up to the northeast. I'm struggling to believe the two things are unrelated."

"They're not," Sasha said. "Our estimates of the planet's natural wildlife have proved way off. I think there's an entire ecosystem contained within the mountain, and possibly on the other side."

"Fabulous," Skerrit said. "And now they're roaming free out here."

"The Yeti is probably an alpha predator," Sasha continued. "Maybe it sees our presence as a challenge. Now that it's exploring new territory, it might be seeking claim."

"It's a natural invader," Naray said.

"It's a son of a bitch," Welker replied. "And I'm looking forward to getting even."

Skerrit raised a hand. "First, I'd like to focus on getting out of here in one piece. Are you handy at all with a wrench and a welding torch?"

"Heck, I use one to keep warm," the corporal said.

"Good. If you're up to it, feel free to give Badejo a hand with the antenna tower. As you know, the beast did a number on it before it chased you out. We need it up and running so we can call a ride from Crown Station. THEN we'll be in a better position to get even with the thing. I'll even tell whatever task force is eventually sent after it to have you go along, if you wish."

That was an answer satisfactory to the corporal.

"In that case, sir, I'll have that thing picking up songs from Earth's radio stations." Welker gave a quick salute, then went out the door.

Skerrit exhaled sharply and walked with Naray to the office, but not before helping himself to a fresh cup of coffee. He took a seat at his desk and allowed himself a moment of peace and quiet.

Naray did the same. It had been an evening of nonstop activity; the polar opposite of what they expected.

"Has there been any progress on the radio?" he asked.

Skerrit took a sip of his coffee before answering. "A little. One of the guys is gonna have to climb the ladder and do some rewiring on one of the panels. But it's looking better than we initially feared. Still have no way of radioing the colony at the moment, obviously. But that might change by tomorrow afternoon."

"Suits me," Naray said. "I'll keep the guys on regular rotations so we have someone on watch at all times. They'll have to sleep sometime. The charges outside the door have been placed. If the beast comes back, it'll be in for a surprise."

Skerrit nodded. "Watch and antenna repair. Those are the two main things." He put his feet up on his desk and rested his eyes for a moment, coffee cup cradled in his hands. "I guess this is what I get for not getting out after eight years."

"Who could have known?" Naray said. "I wasn't thrilled about this assignment either, but I at least figured it beat getting shot at and dodging artillery. Instead of widespread firefights against an enemy army, we're dealing with the Abominable Snowman from the cavern." He looked through the office doorway at Sasha, who was helping herself to a cup of coffee in the kitchen. "Is there a name to that place yet?"

She shook her head. "I'm sure Toby's thought of something. If you ask me, it should be called Death Cavern, since that's all that has come from it."

Naray and Skerrit shared a glance, thought about that, and simultaneously nodded.

No disagreement there.

CHAPTER 9

The time was oh-four-hundred hours. Naray's watch was scheduled to end, but he felt no desire to rotate out. The snooze he had from eleven-hundred hours to oh-two-hundred seemed to have perfectly rebooted him. He was wide awake and fixated on the presence of the enemy. The outside motion detector had not picked up anything so far. Maybe the Yeti had learned its lesson after getting scorched in the explosion.

He doubted it, hence his inability to sleep. Because of that, he saw no point in waking up Pedro, who was scheduled to relieve him. The storm had died down significantly, the air much more bearable now that it was not constantly assaulting him. There was no moon, thus visibility outside the walls was near-zero. It was the closest thing to peace he figured he would get. There was the intermittent beeping from devices and the turning of gears as the satellite dish rotated. That, and the occasional sounds of maintenance from the center of the compound.

His only company came from Roland Welker, who tirelessly worked on the antenna tower. Like the sergeant, he found it difficult to get any sleep either. The corporal was working on a junction box midway up the tower.

A *clang* and a "damn it!" broke the tranquility that had consumed the outpost.

Naray turned around and looked at the tower. He could see Welker in the glow of the work light, looking down at the foot of the tower where his tool had fallen.

The sergeant descended the tight stairwell from the northeast watch post and moved over to the tower. He had intended to get the tool back up to Welker, but the corporal was already sliding down the ladder at a fairly rapid pace.

Welker winced as he touched the ground.

"Oof!" He looked at Naray, slightly embarrassed. "Those painkillers work a little too well. Almost forgot I have a muscle injury."

"Bet you're aware of it now," Naray said. He picked up the wrench and handed it to him.

"That I am," Welker replied, accepting the tool.

While down here, he took the time to check one of the tower legs that had been bent out of proportion during the Yeti's initial attack.

"Having trouble sleeping too?" Naray asked.

Welker sniggered. "Yeah, you're not alone." He used his welding torch to better secure a metal splint he had placed on the leg, casting himself in an orange glow for a minute. He lowered his mask and turned his attention back to Naray. "Frankly, I'm having a hard time sitting still. Maybe it was being trapped under the ridge for over a day."

"That, or you're too pissed to sleep," Naray said bluntly.

Welker shrugged. "There's that too." He looked Naray in the eye. "You don't have a problem with that, do you? Sir?"

There was extra emphasis in that last word. Naray saw through the friendly demeanor. Welker was a timebomb. He had seen many like him during the war. Many guys who had a vendetta against the New Age due to lost friends who were casualties in the war were the worst. It wasn't that they were bad people at heart, but their desire for getting even often interfered with tactical mindfulness. In some cases, it led to hotheadedness and unwillingness to follow orders, turning them into a danger to their allies.

Welker was not quite there yet; he had listened to Lieutenant Skerrit's suggestion without any real fuss. Still, Naray's sixth sense was kicking in.

"Not particularly," he answered. He watched the corporal as he began to ascend the ladder again. "Corporal, it won't be long before we're able to hunt the beast down proper. Who knows? Maybe it learned its lesson today."

Welker stopped and looked down at him. In the bluish reaches of the light was a look of condescension.

"Doubt it. But I guess we won't know, since we didn't stick around to finish the job."

Naray raised an eyebrow at that. "You think we should've chased it down?"

"We had it wounded. The advantage was ours. Something like that wouldn't retreat unless it was vulnerable."

"Or, maybe it wasn't used to being caught on fire," Naray replied. "You saw for yourself how our weapons could barely singe its fur. If we had some rocket launchers, maybe we may have a shot at killing it."

"I guess we'll have to see." Welker resumed climbing the ladder.

Naray said nothing more. There was no point. His suspicions about the corporal were practically unveiled then and there. He would bring it to Skerrit's attention at dawn. For now, it was best to let the lieutenant sleep.

He checked his tablet, which was wirelessly linked to the motion detector. So far, nothing was moving outside of the walls.

"Can't sleep either, huh?"

Naray almost jumped at the unexpected sound of Sasha's voice. She laughed at the sergeant's reaction and extended a cup of coffee she had brought from the Command Post.

"Not really," he said, accepting the coffee.

Sasha sipped from her own mug and watched the sky. "It's crystal clear up there. You can see every star."

Naray looked up. "Yeah, not a bad view."

"I was here for a single rotation during the war," she said. "You could see the ion flares left over from space battles. Remnants of engine cores from Neutron Frigates. Even in space, they burn bright. Basically miniature stars."

"I didn't realize this wasn't your first time on Aguret," Naray said.

"Nope. Second time, though this one has been for a much longer duration," Sasha replied. "It's part of my graduate assignment. Trust me, working in this environment is not my preference."

"Don't think many people prefer this." Naray kept his eyes on the stars. "Then again, I'm not sure what exactly would be suitable for myself, personally. I guess, anything that's not behind a set of bars."

Sasha looked at him and slowly pieced together the meaning behind those words.

"You were arrested?"

Naray took the opportunity to drain some of his beverage. It was a part of his history he was not considerably pleased with.

"Young and dumb, bad crowd, yadda-yadda. Got caught stealing a Drakon fighter from a repair yard. Yeah, they're space fighters, but man are they fast and fun to fly." He laughed. "Worst part was I didn't get to cruise around in the thing before I got busted. Security caught me, and law enforcement picked me up. The war was just getting started."

"Ah." Sasha nodded, understanding what he was getting at. "They said join the army or go to prison. And obviously, you chose the army."

Naray laughed again. "No! I chose prison."

Sasha chuckled in surprise. "Wait, what?"

"You think I wanted to get a gaping hole blown through me? No way. I thought prison sounded better."

"So, what happened?" she asked. "Obviously, you're not in prison now."

"The bombing of Retone happened. Legacy was falling sort of soldiers in that sector, so they told us to either join up or face twenty more years of added-on sentencing. Initially, I only had eighteen months to worry about. As much as I wasn't fond of getting blown up, the idea of rotting in that tin can for two decades seemed worse. A painfully slow death sentence, basically. So, the manipulation worked. I joined up. After the war, I signed on for another term. I've got nothing to go back to, and let's face it, this is keeping me an honest man."

Sasha went to drink, but lowered her cup after that last statement. "Wait? You think you'd go back to your old ways if you weren't in the military?" Naray didn't answer, which in itself served as an affirmation. "Oh, balderdash."

Naray smirked. "Balderdash?"

"Yes. As in rubbish. Drivel. Baloney."

"I know what it means," Naray said. "I just never heard anyone who wasn't eighty years old use that term."

"I'm a geologist," Sasha retorted. "Be lucky I didn't say 'boulder-dash'."

Naray smiled at the bad joke.

"Don't switch careers."

Sasha chuckled in response. "Yeah, you're not the first to make such a suggestion." She looked at the main laboratory module. The interior lights were on. "At least I'm not career-obsessed, like someone I know."

Naray looked in the same direction. "Geez. Does anyone sleep?"

"You and I are at least on alert. Toby, though? He's probably typing up a first, second, and third draft of his report. Trying to secure credit for the discoveries."

"How much longer do you have to work with him?" Naray asked.

"Another eight months," she replied.

"Oof. Looks like you're facing your very own prison sentence."

"That's one way to look at it." Sasha finished her mug. "I guess we all have to make sacrifices for the things we want."

Naray stood quietly. His mind went to what he wanted in life. These past several years, he had been coasting through life, following the routines ingrained in him by the military. Something about his admissions to Sasha made him realize he had no real goals outside staying on the straight and narrow. There was life to be lived. Military service was absolutely honorable, but it was not a life he envisioned for himself. During the war, he solely focused on keeping himself and everyone else alive. Getting to the next day was a nonstop objective.

Only now did he realize that objective was still his driving force, even though he was no longer at war.

BEEP!

Naray lifted his tablet. On the screen was an overhead schematic of Outpost Four and its surrounding acres. From the northeast, a blip was steadily moving towards the perimeter.

"Is that what I think it is?" Sasha asked.

"Probably." He looked up at Welker. "Corporal? Might wanna come back down. We've got company!"

Welker tucked his tool into a bag and slid down the ladder once again. "What's its position?" Naray went ahead and showed him the reading on the screen. "Perfect. It's in range of the turret. I'll go man it."

"Go ahead," Naray said. He turned up the volume on his radio unit and leaned into his mic. "All units, report to the tower. We've got incoming. I repeat, we've got incoming. Bogey approximately three quarters of a mile to the northeast, closing fast."

Lights came on within the barracks and the Command Post. Lieutenant Skerrit's voice came through the receiver.

"On my way, Sergeant. Is anyone on the gun?"

"Welker's on it," Naray responded.

"Welker? You have a visual?"

"Negative, sir," Welker replied. *"I've got the spotlight on."*

Running footsteps from the barracks grew steadily louder. Waterstan, Pedro, Badejo, and Dodger assembled near the radar dish. Beth and George were awake as well, though staying back near the barracks.

Toby Anderson stepped out of the lab module, looking more curious than nervous about the sudden turn in events.

Skerrit approached from the Command Post, having snoozed in his office. He had his rifle resting on his shoulder, fully loaded and ready to fire.

Naray handed him the tablet. Skerrit observed the bogey's position and trajectory.

"Size is consistent with the beast," he said. "I like to think the turret will get the job done. Compared to that, our rifles are party poppers."

"All the same, we should form up on the gate," Naray said. He turned to face the men. "I want a crossfire set up. Forty-five-degree angles. Pedro, Dodger, take the right; Badejo, Waterstan, go left." He looked at Sasha. "Ma'am, I suggest you and your colleagues wait in the Command Post."

"Got it." Sasha sprinted for the barracks and met up with George and Beth. They received the information she relayed and ran with her to the Command Post, stopping near the lab to inform Toby.

Predictably, he had a few snide remarks. Naray couldn't hear the words, but the tone of voice was distinct.

The soldiers took position.

Beyond the walls, heavy footsteps thundered.

Naray checked the bogey's position. "It's coming."

"I've got a visual," Welker said through the radio.

Naray and Skerrit moved to the watch post on the south side of the gate. They ascended the stairwells and stood by the nonfunctional turret, watching the stream of light coming from Welker's position. It swept from the tree line on the north and settled on a large, white figure.

The Yeti had indeed arrived.

"Wait for it to get closer," Skerrit spoke into his mic.

They could hear the whirring of the northeast turret. The beast was watching the source of the light, holding a hand in front of its eyes. It was unused to such strong illumination at night, and probably wondered what this phenomenon was.

Naray watched the beast through a set of binocs. Its left side appeared to have some sort of discoloration in comparison with the rest of its white fur coat. Very consistent with burns. This was the same Yeti that had crashed their gunship.

It was a few hundred yards out, now moving southwards. Welker kept the light fixed on it the entire way, along with the turret barrels.

"It knows we're on to it," Naray whispered to Skerrit.

The beast stopped and looked at the gate. It leaned forward, appearing to squint, possibly taking notice of the barricades. It made one of those laughing noises, deliberately letting its smaller adversaries know what it thought of their efforts to keep it out.

"Yeah, keep laughing," Welker said.

The beast moved closer, still cautious of the blinding light beaming at it. Slowly, its pace increased. Its arms bent at the elbow, the hands closing into fists.

It was ready to burst through the doors and begin its killing spree.

"Welker," Skerrit said. "Go ahead and light it up."

"With pleasure."

A mechanical winding noise resounded from his post. Next, the night air turned orange with a barrage of large blaster bolts.

They struck the ground wide of the Yeti, producing a series of small explosions and a heavy vapor from instantaneously melted snow.

The Yeti jumped to its left and bellowed.

"Son of a bitch."

Welker tried adjusting his aim, but the shots still went wide. The creature moved farther southward, gradually staying ahead from the continuous line of heavy blaster bolts.

Naray knew something was wrong. Welker was a crack shot. No way would he miss this easily.

"What's happening, Corporal?"

"This damn gun! Targeting system is off kilter... aaaaannnnddd... it's already overheating."

The stream of projectiles ceased.

Standing in a sea of thick vapor, the Yeti uncovered its face. It looked at the charred surroundings, then bellowed at the gunner. It was a roar that conveyed many things: You think you can kill me? Who do you think you are? This is MY mountain, sucker!

The roar dwindled into a grunting laugh as the beast moved to the gate. It strutted with confidence. It had ravaged the door when it was fully intact. Little metal splinters welded into a barricade would break like toothpicks under its wrath.

Pounding footsteps grew louder.

The troops maintained position, shivering from both tension and the cold.

"Keep your weapons steady," Naray reminded them. It was also a reminder for himself. Part of him wanted to jump the gun and open fire. But there was a plan in place. The turret failed to take the thing down, leaving their survival on whether the booby trap was a success. Shooting the beast at this point would risk redirecting it to his location.

"You want us? Come get us!" Dodger dared the beast.

It grunted, having heard the voice of the insignificant inhabitant.

By now, it was only ten yards from the gate.

"We're in here!" Pedro shouted. "Come on, you hairy ass-wipe."

"Your mother was a chimpanzee!" Badejo added.

The monster roared in response. No doubt, it understood their sentiments to be a challenge. It pounded its chest like a gorilla, then made its final approach.

The next step touched down less than a meter from the mines.

Red lights came on. The ports yawned open, and three separate spinning projectiles rose from the pucks.

The puzzled Yeti stopped and looked at the spinning things as though they were mosquitoes. They rose to the height of its midsection, their centers blinking rapidly.

All at once, they detonated.

A rolling blast shook the outpost. Pieces of the barricades came loose. A gust of gravel and warm vapor surged over the walls and through the gap in the gate.

Naray rose from cover to get a visual on the target. A plume of smoke and vapor had completely obscured the beast from view. Even Welker's spotlight failed to penetrate the thick curtain.

He heard a moan, and a steady beat of footsteps moving northward. The spotlight panned, catching glimpses of the Yeti as it retreated into the sanctuary of the forest. The blip on the screen disappeared as it moved out of the short range of the motion detectors.

Lieutenant Skerrit took a breath. "It definitely did not see that coming."

The men on the ground raised their guns and began whooping in triumph.

"Oh, yeah!" Badejo shouted. "Serves you right, you ugly motherfu—"

Welker was already on the ground with them. "Why are you all so happy? The son of a bitch got away."

Immediately, the mood soured.

"Um… maybe we're happy because we're not being torn to bits?" Pedro said.

Naray and Skerrit descended the stairwell and met up with the squad right as Dodger threw in a jab at the Alpha Team survivor.

"Well, if you managed to hit the thing, maybe it'd be a different story."

Welker slammed a fist against his own chest in anger, then pointed at the turret with his thumb. "You're not seriously going to blame me for that gun's malfunction?"

"You were here for two months," Dodger said. "You mean to tell me you didn't test it even once?"

Welker squared up with him. "How 'bout I test it now?"

"Hey, hey!" Skerrit yelled. "Stow it. Corporal Welker, cool your jets, damn it." He took a look at the damage to the barricades. The shockwave from the blast had inflicted hell on them, even bending one of the beams out of its original shape.

If such damage could be done to solid metal, how could the flesh and bone of the Yeti have fared?

The newly created space in the barricade allowed the troops to step outside and inspect the blast zone. Welker led the way, rifle at eye-level, even though nothing was in the vicinity. Naray was right behind him, keeping an eye on Welker as much as he did his surroundings.

They formed a circle around the blast point. There, a shallow crater had formed where the mines had been placed. The airburst had kicked up snow for dozens of meters and sent shrapnel pelting the outer perimeter wall.

Flashlights panned everywhere in search of signs of severe injury. The men hoped to find limbs, guts, and as Pedro said, "I'd settle for a severed finger."

They found none of that, but it was not a total loss.

Welker was studying the trail left by the Yeti in its retreat. "I got blood over here."

The others sprinted to his location. Sure enough, warm blood melted holes in the knee-high coating of snow.

Flashlights from the team members extended toward the trees. Sure enough, the bleeding persisted the entire way.

"It's hurt," Pedro said.

"And bleeding profusely," Dodger added. "It's the second time we made that furball run off."

"Maybe now he's learned his lesson," Naray said.

Welker groaned at that remark. "Of course you would think that."

"I agree with the corporal."

All seven soldiers perked up at the sound of that voice. It was not one of their own who chimed in, but rather Dr. Toby Anderson.

The professor stepped through the gate and beheld the sight of the explosive aftermath. "Nice work, gentlemen. We might be on the verge of solving this problem."

"Professor, you might want to head back inside," Noray said.

Toby ignored the suggestion and approached the team, pausing midway to admire the ground zero damage.

"No way that thing will shrug this off. It's got to be on its last leg. Its flesh may be tough, but I think, between the gunship explosion and what just happened here, it's got to have significant injuries."

"Thank you for stating the obvious," Skerrit said. "But, Professor, I would appreciate if you would return to—"

"I think Corporal Roland Welker is correct," Toby continued. "I think you guys are missing a bet here. You've got that thing on the run. For all we know, its guts are hanging out like a Halloween pumpkin that's been carved up. This is our chance! Hell, I'll be your driver. We'll take the cruiser and go after it. Come on! Let's do it now!"

Naray shook his head. "Professor, you've lost your mind. That forest is that creature's turf. We go out there at night, we'll have limited visibility. Our priority now is getting that antenna fixed up so we can evacuate."

"An evac won't do much good if that thing comes back and smashes us all to jelly before the gunships arrive," Toby replied. He had his arms out, speaking with charisma like a politician trying to win over the civilians of a district. "Imagine. If we kill that thing now, we'll be able to sleep through the night, not worrying about delays in our rescue or setbacks in repairing the antenna. But if we let that thing go, it may attempt to retaliate. And how would you keep it out?"

Welker looked at the professor with admiration. It was not clear if he knew Toby was manipulating the situation to enable himself to collect his lost photo scanner, which he desperately wanted to complete his reports. Even if the corporal was aware, it would make no difference. All he wanted was to finish off that Yeti and spit on its corpse.

Badejo raised a hand. "Lieutenant, if I may speak freely?"

"Go ahead," Skerrit replied.

"I think Welker and Professor Anderson are correct. We saw what the beast did to Angelo and our dropship. For all we know, even if we get reinforcements, they might get ambushed in the exact same way. That thing has a hell of a throwing arm, and there's no shortage of rocks or tree branches it could use as projectiles."

"We have our firesticks," Welker added. "Surely, they should be sufficient in finishing the job."

"We can install a plow onto the front of the cruiser," Toby said. "That'll help us move a tad faster on the way into the woods. Certainly will help if we have to make a fast getaway."

"Not a good idea," Naray said.

Skerrit stood quietly. Both sides made sense in this instance. He stared at the blood trail, then looked at the blast point.

"It had to have taken a critical injury," he admitted.

"Sir, we're talking about a beast that can withstand blaster bolts," Naray argued. "Yeah, it's injured, but we can't know the extent. Hell, the thing survived a point-blank fuel explosion and still decided it was up for rampaging through the outpost. Fact is, we don't know what we're walking into out there."

Toby waved him off. "Of course, it could easily return. And with the turret being dysfunctional, there isn't much that'll keep it from coming through that gate."

"We have the manpower and the weaponry," Welker said. "If we don't do something soon, another team may perish. The first instance was a surprise attack. But our deaths are totally preventable. It just requires us to have some balls."

Naray kept his eyes on the lieutenant. The fact Skerrit was giving this nonsense a minute's worth of thought made him sick. Skerrit was a man who based his course of action on whether it was better for the well-being of his men. Often, it was a good trait. Occasionally, it was a detriment.

This was looking to be the latter.

"Alright. We're heading out in five. Do what you need to do. Make sure you're locked and loaded, gentlemen. Let's end this now."

The team returned to the relative safety of the outpost in order to stock up on battery mags and firesticks.

Welker was the last in line, walking alongside Toby Anderson. Neither bothered to give the sergeant a glance as they passed him by. Not that Naray was eager to chat with the two men. One was consumed by vengeance, the other by ego. Both drugs had a similar effect.

"Lieutenant." He stepped in front of Skerrit. The lieutenant was visibly unsure of his decision. Everything was a guessing game. Problem with those was that you had a fifty percent chance of being wrong. And Skerrit knew it.

"We're doing this," Skerrit said. "If that thing comes back, we've got nothing to repel it."

"This is not a good idea, sir," Naray said. "What if our vehicle gets damaged? What if we encounter something else out there? You know the Yeti is not the only thing that came out of that cavern."

Skerrit's jaw tightened. "Sergeant, we HAVE to do this. We don't know how long it'll take to fix that antenna."

"It'll take a hell of a lot longer with less men."

Skerrit knew the sergeant had a point. But the decision was made, and he did not want to complicate matters further by reversing his orders.

"Assign one of the men here as a guard, Sergeant. Then install the plow to the carrier, and be ready to head out in four."

The discussion was over. Naray had plenty of things to say about leaving one soldier here as a guard, as though that would make any difference against that Yeti if it were to show up again. On that note, he was certain the beast would be licking its wounds for the next few hours. Anyone going out there after it was in more danger than anyone staying here. With that in mind, he made his decision on who was to stay.

"Aye-aye, sir."

He saluted and headed into the outpost.

Sasha, Beth, and George were standing a few feet behind the gate, concerned about the drastic course of events.

As soon as she saw the sergeant, Sasha hurried up to him. "Are you guys seriously going out there?"

"Not my call," he said bluntly. "We'll keep one of the guys here to look after you. He'll be able to alert us if the thing returns."

"I'm not worried about us," Sasha said. "I'm worried about you. All of you. Going out there is suicide."

Naray cracked a smile. Nothing about this was funny, but it pleased him to see someone speak common sense.

"I was right. You really would make a good soldier."

Sasha gave a weak smile in appreciation of that compliment. The dread of what the soldiers were facing remained present. And it would until they returned, safe and intact.

"Hey? Sergeant?"

"Yes?"

"Dr. Anderson said something about you punching him."

Naray sniggered. "I take it he was badmouthing me when he brought that up."

"There may be some truth to that," she replied. "Anyway, I just wanted to ask: what did it feel like to hit that stupid asshole?"

Now Naray displayed a wide smile. "It felt great."

Chatter from the Command Post alerted him to the approach of the men. He saw Dodger and Badejo in the front of the line. Behind them was Pedro.

"Hey!" Naray snapped his fingers and got his attention.

Pedro jogged over to the sergeant. "Yeah, boss? What's up?"

"You're staying."

Pedro leaned back as though those words physically struck him on the chin. "Excuse me?"

"You heard me."

Pedro looked down at the gear he was decked out in. “But Sarge? I’m ready to go.”

“I need someone to look after the civilians,” Naray said. “Keep a constant watch. The perimeter motion detectors are still working. We’ll be in radio contact. If you can, tend to the radio tower while you’re at it. If we can get the transmitter fixed, we just might get out of here alive.”

“Is that why you’re keeping me here?” Pedro said. “You’re keeping me alive?”

Naray turned around to go to the garage, initially intending to ignore the question. His better nature took hold, however, and he looked Pedro in the eye.

“You’ve got a kid on the way. Equally as important, it’s looking like there’s actually a snowball’s chance in hell you might settle down instead of banging anything with breasts.”

Pedro perked up, both appreciative and disappointed.

“Any woman of mine would want me to pull my weight and do my duty.”

“She would also want you to come back alive,” Naray said. “Kid too. Trust me, let him have a dad. Don’t let him grow up like me, alright?”

It was a request that also served as a piece of insight into the sergeant’s life that Pedro was unfamiliar with up until now. The words sank deep and flooded his conscience.

“Yes, Sergeant.”

He gave a salute, which Naray returned.

Next, it was time to install the plow. Then they would be off to hunt a Yeti.

CHAPTER 10

As soon as those wheels started spinning, Naray felt himself going mad with the urge to somehow sabotage the vehicle and stop this mission from the get-go. The sight of those trees all around them cemented the reality that they had wandered into the lion's den. Deep down, Skerrit knew this too, but he had allowed himself to be convinced to go on the offensive.

The blood trail remained thick and potent far into the forest. Naray tried to lean on optimism bias. Maybe Welker was right. Maybe the beast was in a vulnerable state. After all, they did not get a good look at the extent of its injuries. Right after the mines had exploded, the beast had retreated. For all he knew, one of its arms could've been dangling by a few strands of meat.

Welker sat on the left side of the middle row of seats. Naray was in the back, carefully watching the window. Toby Anderson was at the wheel. It was another bad call by Skerrit in Naray's opinion. The lieutenant was a good guy, but he was relatively inexperienced in regard to actual combat situations. Most of his time during the war was spent managing stations in noncombat zones. Aside from two brief skirmishes, he was relatively safe from the action. With his career winding down, Naray considered the lieutenant to be one of the lucky ones. But now, he was under pressure. Best of intentions amounted for squat. He was making a bad call, and Naray had no choice but to go along with it.

"It's got to be around here somewhere," Welker said. "I can't imagine it got too far in its condition."

"You don't even know what its condition is," Naray said. He conveyed more than the words he spoke. The contempt in his voice was deliberately broadcast, itself providing a message to the corporal. *You've gone mad. You're gonna get us killed.*

"It took a hit point-blank from three mines," Welker said. "I wouldn't be surprised if we found it dead out here."

THUMP!

The cruiser jolted.

"Whoa!" Dodger said. "Careful there, Doc."

"Sorry," Toby said. "Just because we have the plow doesn't mean we won't hit some rough ground. We're in the forest, gentlemen. There's roots and undergrowth."

"Just take your time," Naray said.

"No way," Welker replied. "Pick up the pace. The more time we waste, the less likely we'll track the Yeti down."

Toby went ahead with the corporal's advice, completely ignoring Naray's higher rank. Skerrit was in the front passenger seat, watching their surroundings with night vision goggles.

"Personally, I can't wait to find that thing," Badejo said. He was sitting next to Welker.

Evidently, the two of them had become buddies when Naray wasn't looking. Badejo was the kind of guy who liked to talk a big game, so it was par for the course he was gung-ho about the hunt.

"I just miss normal outpost duty," Dodger remarked. "And I never thought I'd ever say that."

"Same here," Waterstan said.

"Well, think of it this way, gentlemen," Toby said. "I'll include in my dissertation how you brave men accompanied me in obtaining the greatest zoological find in over a century."

"Is it really that big a deal?" Waterstan asked.

"Oh yes," the professor said. "These creatures have survived in one of the harshest environments known to man. Some of them are related to species that are not adept to freezing conditions. On top of that, they managed to stay in hiding all this time. Meaning, in that cavern, there may be resources that may change the course of human exploration."

Naray snorted. Everything Sasha had told him about the professor was on full display right here. Toby didn't give two shits about what he was rambling about. He probably didn't even believe it himself. He was just practicing his pitch to university boards.

The distraction was nearly enough to make the sergeant notice the lack of prints or blood outside the window.

"Hold up! Stop the cruiser."

Skerrit removed his night vision goggles. "What's going on?"

"Notice something off about our direction?" Naray said, pointing forward.

Skerrit looked straight ahead and caught on to the fact that Toby was no longer following the Yeti's path. "Whoa! Wait a sec. Doc? Did you lose track of where you're going?"

"I'm taking the scenic route," Toby said.

Skerrit sneered. "The hell's that supposed to mean?"

"Just… hold on." Toby was stammering like a teenager who was caught smoking dope. "There's something this way I want to check out. It'll just take a second."

"We're not on a science trip," Skerrit said. "We're hunting a dangerous organism. I only took you up on your offer to drive because I wanted all of my men battle-ready on the turn of a dime."

"And we'll find it. This'll just take a minute. We're almost there."

Skerrit looked at the path up ahead. There were tire marks in the snow. Naray saw it too. They were heading back to the ridge.

"Turn us around," Skerrit said.

"I will," Toby said. His foot applied more pressure to the accelerator. "As soon as I get what I need."

Skerrit shifted in his seat in a manner that could only mean he was about to get heated. Before he could say anything, Toby pointed straight ahead with enthusiasm.

"Here we are."

In the yellow glow of the headlights was the battered gunship. There wasn't much left of it to identify it as an aircraft. At this point, it was nothing but a scrapyard of scattered metal fragments. Some of the pieces were still warming the air, their flames having died out long after the team's retreat.

Toby pulled up to where the cruiser had been parked during the incident, then parked. Before anyone could say anything, he stepped out and began shining a flashlight all over the ground.

Naray followed him outside. "You maniac. You're gonna get us killed. And for what? Some pictures?"

"Relax," Toby said. "The trail veered west a while back. It can't be over here."

"Yeah, but that's not to say we won't run into any rats," Naray said.

"If they show up, you can shoot them," Toby retorted. "You're a soldier. That's what you're paid for." He shuffled through the snow, kicking up huge clumps after finding the collapsible shelter the troops had discarded. The camera unit had to be nearby.

Skerrit stepped out. "Professor!" His voice was a sharp hiss to convey his anger without drawing attention from anything that may be out there. "This was not the plan. I agreed to let you come, but don't think for a second I won't stun your ass and stuff you in the storage compartment."

Toby gleefully reached into a mound of snow, believing to have found his camera. Alas, it was only a chunk of metal.

By now, Dodger, Waterstan, and Badejo were outside. They formed a perimeter while their commanding officer dealt with the science nutcase. Welker stayed inside, completely disinterested in what was going on, and content in the knowledge that they would resume tracking the Yeti once Toby Anderson was appeased.

The professor moved a few yards to the north, then shouted “Ah-ha!” Snow splattered in all directions as the professor ripped the precious device from its burial. Like a paramedic frantically checking the vitals of a patient in critical condition, he brushed all the snow from the cube-shaped device and restarted it. He heard the familiar whirring of mechanical components and the shine of the LED light. “Yes!”

“Good. You have your item,” Skerrit said. “Happy now?”

“Sure am,” Toby said. He turned to head back to the cruiser. “I got what I want. Now, we can get back to our bigfoot hunt and…”

Thump!... Thump!... Thump!...

Everyone froze. Those were definitely footsteps, coming from the northwest. Whatever was making them was big. At least fifteen feet high, judging by the weight behind those impacts.

Skerrit forced Toby to kneel by the vehicle’s rear bumper. “Stay quiet.”

Badejo, Waterstan, and Dodger took firing positions. Night vision goggles were activated and slipped over their eyes. The visitor was approximately seventy meters out, moving slowly.

“Wait a sec…” Naray whispered.

“What is it?” Toby asked.

Naray’s heart started to race. Through the mess of trees, he caught glimpses of the thing’s basic form. It was not humanoid like the Yeti. Though it walked on two hind legs, it was in a forward-leaning pose, almost like a theropod from Earth's Mesozoic Era. Its head resembled that of a Nile crocodile, with huge teeth decorating the edges of its jaws. Two arms were coiled under its torso. They were shorter than the Yeti's, but still long enough to snare and slash prey. The three claws on each hand were more than sufficient enough to do the trick. From the tip of its snout to that of its tail, the thing had to have been over twenty feet long.

Naturally, it was a predator. And it was probably on the hunt.

"Holy shit," Badejo whispered.

They watched as the beast turned its eyes in their direction.

"Shit! Shit! Shit!" Skerrit growled. He rushed to the passenger side of the vehicle and reached across the dashboard in search of the headlight controls. With the twist of a knob, the forwards shut down, coating the team in black air.

Toby shifted near the rear left bumper. "What is it?"

Naray leaned towards him. "Sasha said you guys encountered an overgrown lizard yesterday. Well, we've got one wandering around out there. And based on what she told me, this one is even bigger than the dead one you found."

Toby cringed. "Then why are we sitting here?"

"Shh!" the sergeant hissed. He continued monitoring the threat through his own set of goggles. The beast was moving at a casual pace. If there was any interest in the cruiser's lights, it seemed to have been lost. It moved eastward, stopping occasionally to scratch its head, and at one point getting startled by a clump of snow that fell from a tree.

Everyone remained perfectly still. With a little luck, the thing may just pass them by.

"Once it passes, I want all of you to pile in here," Skerrit whispered, relying on the comms to be heard. "After that, we're heading back to the outpost. Sergeant Naray was right. We're too out of our element here. This was a fool's errand. Just keep still and remain quiet. Pardon the cliché, but don't move a muscle."

The soldiers did exactly that. Rifles remained pointed in the reptile's direction. After several minutes of gradual motion, it was precisely north of their position, still going eastward. It raised its head and sniffed.

A growl rumbled from the back of its throat.

"It smells us," Toby whispered.

"Dude, shut up," Naray said through gritted teeth.

The creature stopped moving and began looking around. More sniffs and another growl struck their nerves.

Toby began inching from his position.

"Don't… move," Naray whispered. He wanted to strike the idiot in the back of the head and knock him unconscious, but doing so would only give away their position entirely.

Now, the reptile was snarling. It raked one of its feet against the ground, then lunged in a burst of motion. A shrieking roar filled the air.

"I'm out of here!" Toby shouted.

“Wait!” Naray went to grab him, but his reach fell short.

The creature tore into the space behind a grove of trees. It was then the sounds of squealing joined the soundtrack of chaos.

Through their goggles, the team watched as the reptile pulled a large rat from its hiding place. It chomped repeatedly and shook its head left to right, spilling blood from the two-hundred-pound rodent. Soon after, pieces fell free, starting with a leg, and eventually the head. The crocodilian leaned up and pointed its snout skyward, allowing the mashed body to fall into its throat.

Headlights came on and the cruiser’s engine roared.

“Hey!” Skerrit shouted. “You maniac! What are you doing?!”

Toby, now in the driver’s seat, floored the accelerator and hooked the vehicle southward down the way they came. The freshly plowed path worked to his advantage, allowing for greater speed. The passenger door flapped like a fish’s pectoral fin as the lieutenant tried to keep himself from falling out while also attempting to stop the panicking professor from abandoning the team.

“Holy shit!” Dodger said. “Not cool, man!”

“Very not cool,” Naray added. He was watching the crocodilian. Drawn by the lights and sound, it turned to its right and quickly began stomping their way. Hiding was a no-go. All they could do was hope for the best. “Run! Run!”

The four men ran after the speeding vehicle. Its rear lights were like stars in the distance, moving back and forth while the vehicle zigzagged. They could hear the horn going off. Skerrit was actively fighting the driver for control.

Finally, the cruiser came to a stop.

It was of little comfort to the team, as it was well over five hundred feet ahead of them. And the reptile was closing in fast.

Realizing this retreat was a death trap, the four soldiers unanimously spun on their heels to engage the approaching monstrosity directly. It closed within thirty feet, arms outstretched, jaws wide open. A stench of minced meat carried in its warm breath as it bellowed at its small challengers.

Blaster fire brought the beast to an abrupt stop. It staggered backwards, its flesh sparking as dozens of burning projectiles made contact. This was its first encounter with such weapons. The heat, the light, and blaring sound of the rifles had successfully stoked a feeling of apprehension.

But like the Yeti, its flesh proved remarkably strong. So strong, it was resilient to blaster fire. Unlike the thick fur coat of the Yeti, this saurian monster had strong, leathery skin, much like an alligator or a snake.

The pause in its attack came to an end. Now that the beast knew it would wade through the hot bullets without taking any significant damage, it moved forward with a booming roar.

Badejo and Waterstan backed away.

"We're in trouble!" the medic said.

Naray looked back at the cruiser. Its engine was revving, the rear lights gradually getting larger.

Skerrit had gained control of the vehicle and was reversing it to their position.

It was a positive change in events that was coming too late.

The sergeant had a split-second to repel the beast. With the blasters insufficient in killing the creature, he figured it was time to give one of those firesticks a try.

He broke the seal and pressed the button inside. The handle protruded from the opposite end.

Naray chucked the explosive at the oncoming reptile. It bounced off its head and flung to the right. Its fuse reached its ten-second limit and ignited its payload. The firestick exploded a few feet from its left heel.

The reptile lurched, slipped on a patch of ice, and came crashing onto its side. Legs pedaled in the air, its tail slapping the ground. An enraged howl from its lungs shook the four men to their core.

They took advantage of the situation and sprinted down the trail. The cruiser was two hundred feet away, skidding against trees and other obstacles as Skerrit closed the distance.

Massive feet touched the ground and lifted the crocodilian upright.

"Dodger! Badejo!" Naray said.

The two soldiers knew what to do. They spun to face the beast and unclipped their firesticks. As their sergeant had done moments before, they cracked the seal and activated the fuse. The handle protruded from the other end. All they had to do now was throw it.

As Naray had said to Sasha Serigami the previous evening, “So easy, a monkey could figure it out.”

Both men chucked their explosives. The timing proved perfect. The firesticks burst in midair, mere feet away from the crocodilian’s face.

It screeched in agony, its eardrums likely rattled by the close proximity of the blast. Smoke billowed from its snout, freshly scarred by heat and shrapnel. Aside from that, the animal was in remarkable condition for having taken near-direct hits from such devastating weapons.

“You’ve got to be kidding me,” Dodger said.

Waterstan grabbed his firestick and broke the seal.

“Wait,” Naray said.

The reptile turned to the east, snarling and shaking its head. The meal in front of it had turned out to be too much trouble. Easier prey wandered nearby.

Two rats, equal to the size of the one it had killed prior to detecting the squad, raced eastward, frightened out of cover by the multiple explosions. The beast broke into a sprint, moving remarkably fast for its size. Gradually, it closed in on the rats and brought its powerful jaws down for the kill.

“First time I’ve ever been happy to see a rodent,” Dodger remarked.

“No shit,” Waterstan replied.

They watched as the reptile brought a foot down on the second rat while still crunching the first in its mouth. It lifted its foot and studied the fresh corpse, savoring the experience of devouring.

Tremors rippled beneath their boots.

Naray looked at the ground, then back at the beast. It was not running, yet the pounding footsteps persisted.

His mind connected the dots—something else was coming their way.

"Holy!" Badejo faced the east and let out a burst of blaster fire.

Low-hanging branches exploded off a nearby tree as the ferocious Yeti emerged. Its hide, lit by the glow of the approaching taillights, was scorched near its left shoulder and center torso, with blood leaking from a gash in the abdomen.

Superficial injuries at most. Not even close to fatal wounds. And given the Yeti's agility, it was ready to get even.

It snatched Badejo off the ground.

"Agh! Get me down!" the soldier shouted. His voice muffled as one of those hands closed over his head and shoulders. The other hand secured a grip over his lower waist, then held the soldier outright like a twig. He was in a straight line, face-up, groaning in utter panic beneath the smelly grip.

The Yeti growled, knowingly performing the act of brutality in front of the other troops.

In one swift motion, it bent the two 'ends' of Badejo downward.

CRACK!

His spine, and everything around it, split. Flesh and blood popped from his center as the two halves of his body came apart.

"Holy God!" Waterstan shouted.

The beast tossed the body parts into the woods, then bellowed at the other men. Its attention went to Dodger. Without skipping a beat, the creature grabbed a piece of broken branch off the ground and whirled its arm around in a throwing motion.

"Whoa!"

True to his name, Dodger dropped into a summersault. His timing proved to be perfect, as the branch came down right where he had been standing.

The cruiser came to a stop. Through its driver's side window, Lieutenant Skerrit shouted at the men. "Get in!"

They raced to the vehicle and crammed themselves through its open doors.

As he awaited his turn, Waterstan made use of the firestick in his hand. He armed the device, gripped it by the handle, then allowed five seconds to pass before throwing it at the Yeti.

It detonated at the creature's feet, successfully driving it backward.

"Get in!" Naray shouted at him.

The medic climbed into the vehicle. Before the door was shut, Skerrit slammed his foot on the accelerator.

Over the next few moments, they watched the Yeti shrink into the distance, looking back at them, equally as pissed as it was when it showed up.

The soldiers caught their breaths. They knew the fight was far from over. The only decent thing that came out of this situation was gaining the knowledge that the beast was very much still in fighting condition.

Toby Anderson was slumped in the front passenger seat, his nose bloodied, courtesy of Skerrit. Welker remained in the same spot, watching through the rear windshield, bitter at the lost opportunity of getting even with the Yeti.

Skerrit glanced at his rear-view mirror at his guys.

“Everyone alright? Wait a minute… where’s Badejo?” The somber silence gave him his answer. “Son of a bitch.” He looked over at the professor. “I ought to blow your knees out and leave you out there for that thing.”

“I’ll volunteer,” Dodger said.

“Hold up,” Toby said. “Anyone would’ve acted the same if confronted with—”

Without taking his eyes off the path, Skerrit plowed a fist into his jaw, shutting the moron up.

As satisfying as it was to watch, it wasn’t enough in Naray’s eyes. Someone else who ought to get a fist to the mouth was Roland Welker. That was an argument that could wait until they returned to the outpost.

For now, the sergeant bided his time and prayed for a miracle.

CHAPTER 11

The sun was initiating its rise as the cruiser passed the gate and parked near the southeast corner. It was a strategic placement, as they knew the Yeti would probably approach from the north and likely go straight for the entrance. With the vehicle on the far end, it increased the odds that the monster would not take the time to smash it up before invading the outpost. If they had to evacuate, their survival was much more likely if they had a ride.

Skerrit pushed Toby Anderson forward as they approached the entrance. The professor grimaced, silently conveying threats of legal action for assault. It only went to show how tone-deaf he was to the situation. His actions had gotten one of Skerrit's men killed. Had he not attempted to flee, the crocodilian would have eventually moved on and they could have returned to the outpost together.

Sasha, George, and Beth were moving between the Command Post and the radio tower. Pedro was up on the ladder, doing some rewiring on the panel. He saw his teammates approach and quickly stepped down to greet them.

"You're back. Did you find it?"

"It found *us*," Dodger muttered.

Pedro's face sank. He looked at the returning teammates, noticing a particular absence.

"It got Badejo?"

Naray nodded. Pedro took a long, slow breath.

Sasha rushed over to the group of soldiers, completely passing Toby by. "You alright?"

Naray replied with an exasperated sigh. "It's not nearly as hurt as we feared. The damn thing survived hits from multiple mines, and all it suffered was some flesh wounds."

"And now we're out of mines," Dodger said. "All it's got to do is walk up and knock."

They gave a punishing look to Corporal Welker as he walked by. Sensing the unspoken meaning behind those blazing eyes, he stopped and faced them directly.

"Blame me all you want. You all wanted to hide in here like a bunch of cowards. We had that piece of shit on the run. For all we knew, the advantage was in our corner."

"If a pack of wolves goes after a rampaging rhinoceros that's way bigger and stronger, it's not courageous," Naray fired back. "It's just plain stupid. That's what going out there was. Stupid."

"Your lieutenant authorized it," Welker said.

"That he did," Naray replied. "At least he had the sense to realize it was a bad plan. If it weren't for your new buddy, we'd all be back here *alive.* And funny, the man calling us cowards seems pretty eager to shift the blame to someone else once a little heat comes his way."

Welker let his weapon strap slide off his arm. He began to unclip his vest. Rank meant nothing. He was ready to settle this right here and now.

"There's some good news," Pedro said. He stepped between the two men and directed their attention to the radio tower. "While you were gone, I was able to make some progress. I replaced the lateral coaxial cable and welded shut the cracked parallel conductor. There's still a little bit of electrical work that needs to be done, but I think we can have it ready shortly."

That was news that had everyone in stunned silence.

Skerrit, who had approached with the intent to break up the altercation between Naray and Welker, managed to crack a smile.

"Wait, you did?"

Pedro stood tall, proud of himself. The usual cocky personality he exhibited before finding out about his baby-mamma situation was on full display.

"Yes sir." He twirled a wrench.

"I didn't know you were so handy," Waterstan said.

"I didn't used to be," Pedro said. "I guess that's one good thing of meeting January. She's part of the electricians team at Crown Station. I was off duty, caught her at work, and thinking I'd make an impression, I thought I'd let her teach me some stuff about her work. Women like being listened to, so I stayed for the entire shift. And stopped by the next day for a repeat."

"Wow," Dodger said. "I guess something good did come out of Pedro's seducing methods."

"Honestly, this is the weirdest start to a relationship I have ever seen," Skerrit said. "But, I'm glad it happened now. Well done, Pedro. Get back at it." He clapped his hands. "Get to work, people. Fix up the barricades. Dodger, get your ass on watch duty. If we play our cards right, we'll be back at the colony by dark."

***

During the course of the next hour, Pedro and Welker worked tirelessly with repairs. Naray kept an eye on the two men through the window of the Command Post. He remained on standby at the radio station with Skerrit. Waterstan was in the infirmary, providing some dental work on Dr. Toby Anderson, who apparently got a cracked tooth during the events off site.

Coffee consumption was constant. Sasha, with nothing better to do, gladly acted as the barista, getting beverages to all of the team members.

She walked up to the radio station and placed a mug on the desk. "Holding up okay?"

Naray accepted the mug. "Just eager to get out of here."

"Can't blame you," she said. "Who knows? You said you saw another one of those reptiles out there. Maybe after you retreated, it and the Yeti decided to drop the gloves and go at it."

Naray chuckled. “I don’t know. Hard to imagine anything other than a neutron bomb breaking through that furry thing’s hide.”

“Ha!” Sasha shook her head and made a tisk sound. “I saw those jaws up close. I can assure you they are designed to crush the bones of animals of similar size. The Yeti clearly doesn’t get along with the crocodilians. Getting the two of them together might just solve our problems for us.” She smiled. “Of course, we can chalk that up to wishful thinking.”

Naray noticed her friendly expression turn sour as she looked over at Toby. It was evident there was more wishful thinking at play. Specifically, a desire to be free of Toby’s so-called guidance.

Pedro’s voice came through the receiver. *“Try it now.”*

Naray put his headset on and pressed the transmitter. “Outpost Four to Crown Station.”

He waited a few moments, but no answer came through.

“Hang on,” Skerrit said. He worked some magic on his office computer. “I’m boosting the signal… okay, give it another try.”

“Outpost Four to Crown Station. This is an emergency broadcast. If you can hear this transmission, please acknowledge.”

Naray and Sasha held their breath.

“Crown Station Zero-Five. I hear you, Outpost Four. What seems to be the problem?”

“Get a senior officer on the horn, pronto.”

“One moment.”

Skerrit pumped a fist. “Nice work, everybody.”

Naray and Sasha slapped hands. She upped the celebration and embraced him in a tight hug.

"Any chance we can celebrate this properly when we get back to the colony?" she asked. "It's been a while since I've been there, but I seem to remember the bar being pretty good."

"One of the few good things about that place," Naray said. "That, and being far away from all the cave monsters."

Sasha smiled. It was a done deal.

"This is Major Jeff Farrow, responding to an emergency call from Outpost Four."

Naray leaned to the transmitter. "Good morning, Major. Good to hear from you."

"What's happening up there? Do you have any knowledge of the whereabouts of Green Line and Alpha Team? They were scheduled to return late last night, but they never showed, and our transmissions have gone unanswered."

"They're dead," Naray said, straightforwardly.

A silent pause preceded the Major's response.

"Dead? What the hell's going on?"

"Listen very carefully, Major…"

CHAPTER 12

The time was thirteen-hundred hours when Naray completed his forty-seventh patrol around the inside perimeter. Though midday, the cloud cover was heavy, making it appear late dusk rather than early afternoon. Dodger was at his usual post, keeping a constant watch of the tree line.

During the morning hours since the radio tower became operational again, Welker and Dodger took the time to replace the turret's battery with the one on the west wall. A few test firings were conducted, and the weapon was good as new.

Snowflakes were starting to come down from the dark grey sky. It started out as a dusting, but gradually intensified.

As much as Naray was looking forward to going home, he was dreading the adjustment it would take. Anything over thirty degrees would feel like living on a sand dune at this point.

Lieutenant Skerrit stepped outside the Command Post and got the sergeant's attention with a wave. "Just got an update from the lead pilot. ETA is roughly an hour."

"We're in the home stretch," Naray said. He saw Sasha standing inside the Command Post through the open doorway. "Roughly nine hours away from trying out that bar."

She beamed a smile at that.

A series of *beeps* from Naray's tablet short circuited the levity. He pulled the device from his side pocket and activated the screen.

Sure enough, a large bogey was coming their way.

"We've got incoming," he announced. "Zero-One-Five. Same as before."

"I see it too," Dodger replied. He rotated the turret to face the threat.

Beth and George hurried out of the main lab, having distracted themselves with their work.

"What's going on?" George asked.

"Get inside the Command Post," Naray said to them. "Stay there until we tell you to come out."

"Yeah?" Toby Anderson emerged from the lab. "Lovely idea. And if that thing forces its way in, what would you suggest then?"

The sergeant swallowed. Even now, the professor seemed to be on a mission to make himself as detestable as possible.

"There's a small sublevel beneath the infirmary," he said. "It'll be tight-fitting, but a few people can stay in there."

"Stay by your radio and we'll tell you what to do," Skerrit said to them before shifting his attention to his troops. "Look alive, people."

Naray and Sasha shared a nod, both conveying the same message to one another.

Be careful.

The sergeant ascended the northeast stairwell to join Dodger at the watch post. On the screen, the blip drew closer to the tree line.

Dodger cackled with a heavy aura of confidence. "Dumb ape. Obviously it didn't learn from last time. It thinks it can just walk right on up and kick in the door. As if we won't blow it to pieces before it gets anywhere near the door."

"Let's be sure that's what happens," Naray replied. "That gun still working?"

"You saw the tests."

"I did. I also know how our weapons tend to go bad whenever they feel like it. Which also tends to occur right when we need them the most."

Dodger shook his head. "You'll see in just a moment. Once that bad boy shows his ugly face, he'll be met with…" He looked at his own monitor. "Wait. What the hell is this?"

Naray glanced at the screen, and ended up giving a similar reaction.

The blip had broken apart into a dozen smaller individual readings. Like an invading army, they tore from the tree line into the clearing.

Rats.

They moved in an unorganized frenzy. The only semblance of coordination was the fact they were moving south. Like a pack of wolves, they stopped and sniffed, detecting the faint odor of burnt fuel.

Dodger scoffed.

"You've got to be kidding me."

"What's going on?" Skerrit called up to them.

"Rats!" Dodger replied. "A lot of them."

He wasn't taking any chances; shifting the gun to the right, Dodger unleashed a volley of energy bolts onto the small herd. The rats squealed in panic and veered off to the east. Dodger kept up the punishment, reducing a few of the fleabags into smoldering mounds of flesh.

An odor of charred meat drifted in the wind.

The other rodents resumed their retreat into the east tree line and gradually disappeared into the forest.

Dodger ceased fire. Lifting his eyes from the electronic crosshairs, he started to laugh.

"Well, that was a tad underwhelming."

Naray was still going over what had happened in his mind. "The pack must've been tightly grouped together. Though, I don't understand how they stayed close together. It was almost as if they were trying to resemble one large predator and…"

Beep!

Both men looked to the motion tracker. A large blip approached from the northeast… the exact same spot from where the pack of rats dispersed from.

Another small blip moved from the large reading. It moved directly at the watch post at a rapid speed.

Naray noticed the round shadow crossing the landscape, and the huge rigid spherical shape arching high above it. It was an all-too-familiar object, coming at them like a meteorite, much like the boulder that had struck the gunship less than twenty-four hours ago.

Dodger saw it too. For once, he did not live up to his name.

His upper body burst like a red water balloon as the huge piece of rock connected with him.

Naray fell against the guardrail, shook by the tremor of impact that obliterated his teammate as well as the turret. Body parts and mechanical components fell from the watch onto the stairwell.

Waterstan stood up from his defensive position near the gate. "What the—"

Down below, the squad nearly broke formation after seeing pieces of Dodger coming off the wall.

Naray gathered his composure and got a read on the situation. The turret, the last weapon in their armament with any chance of doing any significant damage on the Yeti, was wrecked.

The huge white beast emerged from its hiding spot, grunting like an ape in triumph after seeing the red stains resulting from its recent kill. Its left hand was cupped near its torso, as though cradling something. Moving in closer, the beast picked up something that, in comparison to its huge hands, resembled a black raisin. It touched the object to the tip of one of its canines, then tossed it over the wall.

It reeled over Naray's head and touched down near the base of the radar dish. There, Naray and everyone else was able to get a better view of the thing. It was shaped like a hockey puck, with a metal rod protruding from one end, and a busted seal on the other where a trigger had initiated an internal fuse.

A firestick.

Naray's heart skipped a beat.

So easy, a monkey could figure it out.

Or a Yeti...

A tremendous blast consumed the base of the dish. Shrapnel and flames expanded from the epicenter, shifting the large device as well as the nearby radio tower.

Now, the men broke formation.

"What the hell's going on?" Pedro said.

Numerous realizations came to Naray's mind at once, including the origins of the firesticks and how the beast understood how to use them. The latter was explained by the fact it had witnessed the troops using the firesticks during the night, both when they repelled the crocodilian, and when Waterstan used one against it. Over the course of the next several hours, it had gone back to where the members of Alpha Team lay and collected the explosives from them, all with the intent of putting them to its own use.

The beast was closer now, still cradling several more firesticks in its left hand. It armed another one and tossed it over the wall.

Naray followed the trajectory of the small black object, right up until it landed right in front of the three troops on the ground.

"Withdraw!" he shouted.

Waterstan, Pedro, and Welker saw the thing and quickly sprinted to the interior of the compound.

BOOM!

"AGH!"

Before anyone could realize what happened and who went down, more firesticks were tossed over the wall. One exploded by the dish. The other somewhere to the south.

An alarm blared.

Naray looked south through the clouds of smoke at a set of red strobe lights near the southwest section.

"Oh no…"

He ran down the stairwell and linked up with Skerrit, who was running in the direction of the fallen soldier.

It was Waterstan who had been tossed by the second explosion. The medic was on his back, smoke wafting from his tattered battle suit.

Pedro and Welker hurried over to him as well.

"Hang on, Doc!" the former said. "We'll get you to the infirmary." He looked at the others. "Let's lift him."

"I'll help you," Skerrit said. "Sergeant! Get a look at the reactor. How badly damaged is it?"

Naray broke into a sprint and moved the several meters of distance between the gate and the power station. A small crater marked the ground by the unit's easternmost side. The outer shell had been severely cracked, and from within those breaches came hot white fumes.

His eyes went to the two cooling towers and the water pipes. Water was free-flowing onto the ground, melting the snow all around it. The pipe had been severed in the blast. Already, the effects of the constant cooling cycle was being felt.

"Shit!" He went to the control panel. It too had suffered damage.

He tried to shut down the reactor, but the buttons had been reduced to pieces of orange plastic squares. They were useless.

"How's it coming over there?" Skerrit called to him.

"Lieutenant, we need to evacuate," Naray shouted back. "The reactor unit has taken a direct hit. The pipe's completely busted. I can't shut it down. We've got forty-five minutes—at best, an hour—before it blows."

Skerrit pointed at Welker. "In the garage, we can weld together a new section of pipe and—"

BAM! BAM! BAM!

Chunks of metal spat from the barricades. The door itself folded back gradually, the entryway widening as the Yeti pounded the gate. It hammered its fist, folding the edge of the door inward, and with one final body slam, it broke the entire thing off the rail.

It had breached the perimeter.

Right away, it set its sights on the four men in front of it.

Pedro and Skerrit held their ground, refusing to abandon the injured medic, despite his urging for them to run. Welker, for all of his tough talk, was more than happy to backpedal and use the other soldiers as an opportunity to get away.

"Guys! Move!" Naray shouted.

Pedro and Skerrit opened fire on the creature. It marched up to them, taking the brunt of their gunfire without so much as a flinch.

It raised its right hand to its left shoulder, then swatted. The back of its wrist connected with Pedro, sending him far off the ground like a golf ball. He landed nearly twenty feet away, his gun bouncing end-over-end towards the Command Post.

A swatting motion from the opposite arm struck Skerrit. He reeled backward, settling facedown a few yards from Naray's position. Blood spat from his mouth and the pain of broken ribs and ruptured internal organs was immediate.

The beast approached Waterstan.

He lay on his back, firing frantically while screaming in hysterics.

"Get away from me, you big ol'—"

The Yeti raised its foot and brought its heel down on his head. Hands and legs spasmed as the body's organic computer system was grounded into pulp.

It lifted its foot, peeling strands of brain and skull from the red snow. Unsatisfied with ending its killing spree here, it turned its eyes to Lieutenant Skerrit.

Naray rushed to his side and sat him upright. "Sir, now's not a good time to stretch out."

Skerrit grunted in pain and slammed a fresh battery mag into his rifle. The ground rumbled as the Yeti plodded in their direction.

"Sergeant, save the civilians," Skerrit said.

"But sir!" Naray knew the hidden meaning behind the words was 'leave me here'.

Skerrit grabbed him. "You're not the man you were before you signed on, son. You're the best of us. That's why I trust you to save them. It's what we do, soldier!"

He pushed the sergeant away and shouldered his weapon. The Yeti was nearly on top of him now. A blaster bolt struck the corner of its eye, causing the beast to stumble backward.

It extended its jaws for an incensed roar.

Skerrit concentrated his fire, landing a blaster bolt right against the soft flesh on the roof of its mouth.

The Yeti stumbled back again, spitting blackened blood and burnt skin.

"Taste good?" Skerrit said.

Naray, having followed his orders, moved to the south lab module. As he reached its entrance, the Yeti made a second approach to the lieutenant.

Skerrit kept the gun spraying at the beast right up to the very moment it picked him off the ground and wrapped its hand around his head. Its fingers tightened into a fist.

A resounding *ccrrrraaaacckkk*, coupled with the dripping of blood between the Yeti's fingers induced a ping of nausea in Naray's stomach.

The beast tossed Skerrit's body aside and looked around for the sergeant. As soon as it spotted him at the lab module, it charged.

Naray threw himself to the back of the small building and braced for the upcoming impact. The front wall imploded, throwing lab supplies and machinery all over the floor. Enormous hands reached through the doorway and pulled in opposite directions. The walls split apart, widening the doorway.

It put its face through the large gap and bared its ugly smile at Naray.

He pointed his weapon, only to be knocked backwards as one of those huge hands came at him.

Its grasp missed him, but managed to seize his rifle and crush it in its palm.

The Yeti looked at the scrap metal that used to be the rifle, then discarded it. It reached into the module a second time, brushing away the center workstation that Naray hid behind. A cruel apex predator who delighted in the harm it caused, it taunted Naray with another smile. That giant right hand opened up and came at him.

Naray closed his eyes and prayed for a quick death.

Behind its shoulder came the flash of blaster bolts and the sparks from their impact against its hide. The Yeti reared its head back and roared, pivoting on its feet to look at the source of the pesky attack.

Sasha yelled, firing Pedro's rifle from across the compound. Behind her, George and Beth picked up the injured soldier and began dragging him to the Command Post.

More shots struck the beast. Sasha proved to be a natural markswoman with the weapon, landing a few shots on its face and neck. Succumbing to its violent temper, the creature abandoned its attack on Naray in favor of slaughtering her.

"Hurry! Hurry! Run!" Sasha yelled at the others. Together, they retreated into the Command Post.

Naray raced out of the wrecked lab, ready to stop the beast with his bare hands. It was well out of reach, heading straight for his new friends.

Knowing they had Pedro's radio, he used his radio to contact them.

"Get in the storage compartment and shut the hatch. Hurry! The thing doesn't know there's a sublevel. It'll think it lost you."

"Doing it now," Pedro groaned in reply. Naray could hear the hatch door yawning open. After a moment, Sasha took the radio from him.

"Sergeant, are you alright?"

Naray clenched his teeth, watching the beast ram into the Command Post. Sasha gasped into the mic.

Toby Anderson's voice was easily heard. *"This is suicide!"*

"Shut up!" Sasha said to him. *"Naray? Are you okay?"*

"I'm fine," he said. He looked around and began strategizing. He was out of effective weapons. The turrets were useless and he was out of explosives. Even if he wasn't, using them so close to the Command Post would be as much of a danger to the survivors as the Yeti.

Think, damn it, think!

Anger flooded his body. They were so close to escaping, only to be torn apart in the home stretch. There was no more fear. He was ready to run across the compound, throw himself onto the Yeti, and fight with the natural weapons God gave him. Fists, feet, teeth…

He froze, gripped by a new thought.

Teeth…

Maybe there was a weapon at his disposal after all. He just needed to go out there and find it.

"It couldn't have gone far from where we found it last night," he said to himself. "I bet if I took the cruiser out there and blared the horn enough times, it'd be like ringing the dinner bell."

There was only one way to find out.

He sprinted for the open gate, yelling into his mic. "Sasha, stay where you are. I have an idea. Do you have a motion tracker?"

"Pedro has one."

"Keep an eye on it. If the creature leaves, then get out and go as far south as you possibly can. If it stays, do not move."

"What are you going to do?"

"Recruiting some backup."

When he arrived at the gate, the Yeti had ripped off the west side of the Command Post. It peered through the newly-created opening and peered inside. Instantly, the confusion was evident. The humans had seemingly disappeared into thin air.

Naray breathed a sigh of relief. As intelligent as the Yeti was, it was unfamiliar with the concept of basements.

That relief reverted to terror as that big ugly face turned towards him.

"Oh, shit."

A tremendous roar shook him to his core.

Naray ran through the snow, simultaneously happy and perturbed that Skerrit had parked the cruiser so far out of the way.

He heard its engine ignite.

"What the…"

The headlights came on. Seated on the other side of the window was Corporal Roland Welker.

The formerly gung-ho soldier was ready to run with his tail between his legs. It would not have been so big a deal in Naray's mind if the guy wasn't attempting to turn the vehicle south.

"Don't you even think about it!"

Welker glanced at the sergeant and shook his head. He put the vehicle in reverse and put it against the perimeter wall. He shifted into forward gear, the wheels turned to the right.

Naray threw himself against the cruiser and rammed the handle of his knife against the window. Glass shattered over the driver.

"You maniac!" Welker shouted.

"Yeah? Think you were just gonna take off without us, huh? What happened to all the tough talk?"

The corporal responded by elbowing him in the face, then stomped on the accelerator.

Naray reached into the window, shards of glass in the frame cutting into his arm. As he was dragged through the snow, he reached for the inner lock and unlatched the door.

"Damn you!" Welker shouted.

Naray opened the door and grabbed the corporal by the collar. With Welker not being buckled in the seat, it only took a big yank to pull him out of the vehicle.

Welker hit the snow and rolled, the vehicle continuing to move several yards away. Naray pulled himself into the driver's seat and redirected the cruiser northward.

The Yeti emerged through the gate.

Welker stood up and faced the giant. He had his sidearm in hand and was debating whether to use it on the sergeant or the beast.

It ended up being the latter, and ultimately a futile effort.

"Eat this, you son of a bitch!" he shouted. He plucked his firestick from his vest and armed it.

As he went to throw it, the Yeti closed the distance. Welker was snatched by the midsection and lifted eighteen feet high.

With its other hand, the Yeti grabbed his right arm and pulled it from its socket, stretching strands of flesh and tendons.

Welker roared in agony, watching his arm separate from the rest of him. Having recognized the explosive device still in the dead hand's grip, the Yeti tossed it into the woods, where it detonated harmlessly.

The beast held Welker close to its face, watching the blood pour from his arm socket. The corporal, getting woozy, gave one final act of defiance by spitting in its face.

"Fuck you!"

The Yeti parted a grin, then simply squeezed its hand.

Welker squirmed in its tightening grasp. Ribs, hip bones, and after a few seconds, his spine snapped. The grasp continued to tighten, squeezing Welker as though he was a lime. Blood spurted from every orifice, including his mouth and ears.

In the end, the creature dropped him, leaving behind a crumpled, imploded version of the once-feisty soldier.

As it turned its attention back to the cruiser, Naray was far into the woods.

Glancing repeatedly into his rear-view mirror, he hoped the Yeti would follow him and give the others a chance to make distance from the reactor before it exploded. Alas, it appeared it was keen on claiming the outpost as part of its territory.

***

For minutes, he traveled through the woods, blaring his horn like a man with road rage. A few birds and furry critters moved about. Occasionally, he saw a rat.

"Come on, I know you're out here." He stopped the vehicle and stepped out. Using Welker's rifle, which had been left in the passenger seat, he fired several shots in the air. "Come on! I know you're still hungry! Come out and get me!"

It successfully drew the attention of a carnivorous visitor—a six-foot rat. Dragging its fat belly over the snow, it moved around a tree and approached the soldier, baring its pointy teeth.

"Oh, for heaven's sake!"

Naray removed the threat with a shot to the head.

He checked the time. It had been eighteen minutes since he departed. There was maybe twenty-five—at best, forty minutes until the reactor would explode.

It seemed hopeless. He had convinced himself he could find the crocodilian. Now, he was realizing the stupidity of his plan that was born out of sheer desperation. Finding a specific lifeform in all of this mountainside was truly a needle-in-a-haystack venture.

He blared the horn some more, out of defiance, if nothing else.

Stomp! Stomp! Stomp!

A husky bellow came from the same direction.

Naray turned to the northeast. Through the trees, the elongated bipedal form emerged. The crocodilian approached in the exact same movements as a tyrannosaurus in a blockbuster movie from the early 21st century. The jaw hung open, exhaling warm air.

Naray fired a few more shots into the air.

"Yeah, that's right, come on over."

Enticing the beast further, he directed some of those blaster bolts in its direction. One of them managed to strike its neck, elevating its mind from curiosity to full-blown anger.

Hearing the ear-piercing roar, Naray took the hint. He threw himself into the driver's seat and turned around.

With the crocodilian right behind him, he floored the pedal and went south for Outpost Four.

CHAPTER 13

"I'm telling you, he saved his own skin!"

Sasha couldn't take Toby's voice anymore. Up until yesterday, she had barely managed to tolerate his egotistical behavior day in and day out. Her academic and professional career depended on it.

At one point in her life, she considered herself to be highly ambitious. In the beginning, she was able to relate to the professor's obsessive ways. But now, she saw the effects of one who buried himself in his ego and ambition. Toby had nothing outside of his work. Not a hobby or a loved one. Any family he had was put to a literal and figurative distance as he trekked across the galaxy, hoping to make a name for himself.

Having goals and ambition was one thing. Pursuing it at the cost of everything else was something else. It isolated him, forging a view of people as little more than objects to be used and disposed of. Hence, his current rant about Sergeant Naray supposedly abandoning them.

Sasha refused to let herself fall into that trap.

"He's coming back."

"Ha!" Toby's laugh was borderline psychotic, perfectly matching the wide-eyed expression. "Right? Why? There's nothing here for him to come back to. He's got the cruiser. The reactor is in critical condition. If he had half a brain, he'd be ten miles away already."

"Why?" Sasha said. "Because that's what *you* would do?"

Toby leaned over Pedro and shifted the tablet screen in her direction. "Take a look! You see that big ol' blip moving inside the perimeter? That's the Yeti! Yeah, he's gone."

Pedro, enduring the pain of his fractured ribs, pushed the professor back to his side of the storage compartment. "Get off me!"

Toby hit the wall, then raised a hand, tempted to retaliate. He then remembered Pedro was the one with a pistol on his hip, and reconsidered his course of action.

"So close, yet so far," he muttered.

Sasha knew what he meant. The statement had nothing to do with their survival, but rather about reaching his lifelong goal of a grand discovery, and the fame that would hopefully come with it.

If Sasha had her way, she would drop a bomb on that cavern entrance and seal it permanently.

George and Beth were huddled on the south end of the room, speaking silently in prayer.

"Oh, how cute," Toby remarked.

Pedro and Sasha scowled at him.

"For real?" the soldier exclaimed. "They're seeking comfort and also asking for a miracle, and you're mocking them?"

"Just find it hilarious," Toby said. "I mean, what a way to go out."

"Like what you're doing is so dignified?" Sasha replied.

"Hey, at least I'm keeping it real," Toby said. "I'm not leaning on false hope that the soldier boy you've developed a crush for will suddenly come back with a method for getting us out of this mess."

Beep!

Sasha and Pedro looked at the tablet.

"We've got incoming from the northeast," he said. "Two bogeys."

"Two?" Toby shook his head. "Great. Now we're really screwed." He looked at Sasha, who was smiling ear-to-ear. "And may I ask what has you glowing so brightly?"

Sasha put her hand to the ceiling, feeling the influx of tremors gradually intensifying as their new visitor approached.

"Naray did it. And he brought backup."

***

The Yeti was in the middle of tearing apart the radar dish when it heard the familiar sound of the cruiser's engine. Sensing that the one human who had gotten away was returning, it turned around and watched the entrance. As it waited zealously for the foolish human's arrival, it sensed the presence of an entirely different foe. Its heightened sense of smell detected the fishy odor of scaly skin.

Its hairs raised on end. In the blink of an eye, its interest in the pitiful human had vanished, for a species it despised all of its life had dared show its face in its newly-won fortress. A day ago, it had encountered a young adult member and took great pleasure in breaking its neck.

For all of its life, it had been at war with the crocodilians. Whenever it found a nest, the Yeti took great pleasure in either stomping them outright, or cracking them open and enjoying a little breakfast—directly in front of the parent, if the opportunity presented itself.

Sounds of thunder and the growling engine neared the opening. The headlights shined their bright luminosity into the fully breached entryway. Bouncing over metal fragments, the vehicle entered the compound.

Behind it came the crocodilian beast.

The Yeti stepped back, its aggression paused by a brief sense of alarm. Standing before it, the pale-skinned, long-jawed reptile came to a stop, abandoning its pursuit of the human after laying eyes on the mammal. It was certainly bigger than the last one the Yeti had encountered. Standing in its typical stance, the crocodilian matched the Yeti in height. In terms of overall body mass, it held an advantage.

The Yeti was not concerned. It was no stranger to violent brawls with the various beasts in its original ecosystem. Anything that had lived north of the mountain endured an existence of pain and violence. It was the only way to survive. As the Yeti had learned, developing a bone-deep hatred for its rivals fueled its fighting abilities.

A similar hatred was conveyed through those eyes. As hungry as the crocodilian was, it did not see the Yeti solely as food. The glory of slaughtering the huge furry beast would be a reward in itself. Consuming its flesh would just be a bonus.

It parted those mighty jaws and roared its challenge.

The Yeti bared its ugly grin in response. It threw its arms wide and leaned forward, daring the crocodilian to make its move.

As anticipated, the reptile charged.

The Yeti sprinted, bellowing a lifetime of rage.

The two beasts met in the middle with an earth-shaking *CRASH!*

A cyclone of teeth and claws created a blur of motion and a persistent flow of seismic activity underneath the compound.

***

Naray parked the cruiser near the Command Post and rushed inside. He took in the sight of immense rubble that used to be the module.

"Sasha! Pedro!"

BAM!

He jumped at the sound of the two beasts hitting the ground at once. The Yeti had the crocodilian in a headlock and was trying to work itself into a position where it could crack its neck. The reptile pedaled its legs, initially catching nothing but air, until finally its sharp toes caught the Yeti's left knee.

Yelping in pain, the simian beast released its grasp and stood up. The crocodilian, still on its side, cocked its leg, then rammed its foot into the Yeti's pelvis, successfully driving it backwards.

Naray held his microphone close to his lips. "Sasha? Pedro? Are you there?"

Another voice came through the receiver.

"Whiskey-Charlie-Five to Outpost Four. Is anyone on Bravo Team on this channel?"

"This is Sergeant Naray. Please tell me this is the flight team."

"There you are. That's affirmative, Sergeant. We are only three miles out, getting ready to make our final approach. We haven't been able to reach you guys on the station's channel..."

"Yeah, because the place has been wrecked! You'll understand when you get here," Naray said. "Listen guys, our reactor has gone critical. Any additional aircraft needs to turn back now. Whoever picks us up needs to land on our flight deck. It's clear and set to go."

"What? How long until it blows?"

"Minutes," Naray said. It took everything not to lie and give the impression they had more time, but it had already been forty-five minutes since the cooling system failed, and he was not going to deliberately get someone else killed. He closed his eyes and hoped whoever was on the other end of the channel was someone with balls of steel.

"I'm making my approach. If you're not on that deck when I arrive, I'm turning around."

"Thank you!" Naray ran into the Command Post, hopping over pieces of ceiling and what used to be the galley as he made his way to the hatch.

A faint voice could be heard from under the floor of the infirmary. "Naray!"

Now it made sense why they had not surfaced. A piece of rubble from the overhead had fallen on the hatch door and jammed it shut.

Using every ounce of his strength, Naray pushed the big slab of metal aside.

The hatch door swung open. Out came Sasha, holding Pedro's rifle in hand. She gave Naray a hug and a kiss on the cheek.

"Oh, thank God you made it."

He shrugged. "Well, we still have that date, right?"

Smiling at that, she helped George and Beth push Pedro out of the hatch. Moaning in pain, he gave a half-assed salute to the sergeant.

"Glad you made it."

"Not letting you get out of your new responsibilities," Naray quipped. "Come on. There's a pretty woman and a bundle of joy waiting for you. By the way, everyone, we're in a rush. Our ride's on the way, and if we're not at the bus stop, we're SOL."

Taking that warning seriously, everyone ran through the Command Post as fast as they could. As they moved to the west edge of the building, where the cruiser was waiting and running, more rubble rained from the overhead. The ground was rumbling endlessly while the two giants outside continued their violent brawl.

Naray and Pedro stopped in their tracks, narrowly avoiding a large chunk of debris. Behind them, Sasha and George were not so lucky. A massive slab of ceiling came down on top of them, driving the two scientists to their knees.

Naray and Pedro turned around and joined Beth in a hasty effort to get them to their feet.

Seizing the opportunity, Toby Anderson sprinted past them. Tucked under one arm was his portable computer which held his precious reports. Under the other was his camera unit with the photographs of all of his findings.

He hurried outside and turned the corner.

"Doctor!" Sasha shouted, realizing what he was up to.

It was not just about the glory of fame and fortune now. Toby knew he was facing a tribunal for his actions on the field which resulted in Badejo's death. If everyone was dead, nobody would be able to testify, and the whole thing would be left unknown to everyone in the galaxy except himself.

Naray sprinted after him. "You son of a bitch!"

Toby was climbing into the passenger seat as the sergeant turned the corner. The door slammed shut and the wheels began spinning. Naray reached for the vehicle, only for it to race south.

Cursing, he watched the cruiser speed along the wall, straight for the exit. Toby deliberately had the window down for them to hear his laughter.

"See ya, suckers! HA! HA! HA!... AHHHH!!!"

Absorbing the impact of a forward charge, the Yeti reeled backward, landing directly in the path of the cruiser.

It smashed against its shoulder, drawing a shriek from the huge Yeti. The rear of the vehicle came up, and out through its windshield went a bloodied Toby Anderson. He summersaulted across the beast's chest, settling on his back. Despite the pain and disorientation, he quickly recognized he was lying across in the Yeti's fur coat. He scrambled to his feet in a frenzy and attempted to leap to safety, only to find himself wrapped in the Yeti's grasp.

With his arms pinned to his sides, Toby wiggled and yelled.

"Put me down! Put me down!"

The Yeti got back on its feet and faced off with the crocodilian, human in hand. The reptile crouched, sized up its opponent, then lunged for a bite.

In a calculated motion, the Yeti sidestepped, avoiding the clamping of those jaws. Like a black ops professional with a knife, it rammed its weapon into the enemy's right eye. Toby's upper body splattered over the crocodilian's face, blinding it under a fog of blood and guts.

The reptile roared and attempted to back away, only for the Yeti to press the attack. It landed a punch to the nose before putting all of its bodyweight into a tackle. Together, both creatures crashed into the remains of the radar dish.

Naray looked over his shoulder as the others stepped out of the Command Post. They took in the sight of the wrecked vehicle and experienced a moment of despair.

"Come on!" he shouted at them. "We're not licked yet."

As soon as he spoke, they heard the engines of a gunship descend from the heavens.

"Sergeant Naray, I'm not seeing you on that flight deck."

"We're in the perimeter! Near the Command Post," Naray replied.

"We can't wait, Sergeant."

"For the love of God, man! Just swing over here and drop the ramp! You've got space! Now hurry! There's civilians here! One of our guys has a girl back home who's pregnant."

"Ugh! We're dropping the ramp. You guys better fly inside as soon as I touch down."

There was a whine from the engines, followed by a downward draft from the rotors as the gunship passed over the wall. The pilot hesitated before setting down, obviously alarmed by the sight of the two predators locked in combat.

"Holy shit! What are those things?!"

"We'll tell you on the way back," Naray said.

The dropship came down, its ramp yawning open. Staying true to their promise, the team of survivors climbed aboard and found a seat. The crew inside helped the injured Pedro aboard and clipped his harness on.

Naray was last to step aboard. He hit the manual control for the ramp to raise it, then took a seat on the starboard side next to Sasha.

"Hit it!"

On the other side of his window, the beasts were lost in the fog of battle, neither taking notice of the large aircraft until it had ascended high into the sky.

The Yeti sneered. Those crafty little creatures had managed to get away. Rarely did any victim ever manage to escape its wrath.

Its distraction cost it the leverage it had over the crocodilian. A smack of its long tail knocked the Yeti backwards. Rising to its feet, the retile sprang. Its jaws slammed shut over the Yeti's left forearm. Teeth drove deep into the flesh, the immense pressure testing the integrity of the bones underneath.

Rearing its head back, the Yeti roared. It hammered its other fist against its enemy's face, failing to loosen its grasp. Punching it in the neck and ribs proved equally futile.

The crocodilian, applying additional pressure, jerked its head in a counterclockwise motion.

SNAP!

A tsunami of pain surged from the broken forearm through the rest of the Yeti's body.

The odds were shifting from its favor, and the beast knew this. It was a reality it refused to face, as the Yeti was fueled by the same driving force of the other dominant species on this planet—Ego.

Death was a certainty, for the beast had no delusions of immortality. But it would be damned if it allowed its reign to end because it was bested by a godforsaken crocodilian of all things.

It looked to its left. Lying in the snow were the bodies of the soldiers it had slain less than an hour earlier. Allowing the reptile to maintain its grasp, the Yeti backpedaled towards the corpses. The Croc went with its enemy, not wanting to relinquish its grasp, and believing the motions to be a form of retreat.

Now standing over one of the corpses, the Yeti reached down and plucked the small black explosive from the outer layer of clothing. It rammed the hollow component against the tip of one of its teeth, causing the small silver rod to eject. Knowing it had a few seconds left before the painful burst, it used its broken arm to tilt the crocodilian's head upward.

It slipped the object between its teeth and let it fall into the back of the reptile's throat. Wrapping its good arm around its opponent's neck, it held the Croc in place.

BOOM!

An eruption of blood spewed from the crocodilian's mouth. Its torso bloated and its neck split open, spilling portions of its tongue and esophagus onto the snow. The jaws limply hung open, and the once-powerful theropod collapsed face-first into the snow.

The Yeti stood over the corpse of its foe, panting, in considerable pain, but all in all, triumphant.

It pounded its good arm against its chest and roared to the heavens.

The humans may have gotten away, but it had been successful in claiming their fortress. Now, this territory belonged to it. It was victorious, consumed in the high of its achievement, completely unaware of the surprise its new home had in store for it.

It took notice of what appeared to be blue lightning bolts expelling from a rectangular object to its right. The Yeti stared, confused, unsure of what the phenomenon was.

Next, it found itself consumed by a world of bright light and unbearable heat.

***

Naray covered his eyes as the blast illuminated the horizon. A shockwave swept through the forest, bending the trees and causing rockslides and avalanches on the steeper locations. The white shine shrank, and a thunderball of red fire took its place.

Jittering in their seats, everyone remained silent and hoped for the best as the gunship fled south.

After a few moments, silence took over.

The pilot relayed the incident over the radio to Crown Station, his transmission ending with *"...but we just managed to get out of range. We have the survivors. We're heading back now."*

Naray took a breath. It was over.

He felt Sasha's hand close over his.

"Thanks for coming back," she said.

He smiled. "Like I said, I had a date."

They kept their hands together and watched the landscape pass by as they moved on to better horizons.

The End

Check out other great

Cryptid Novels!

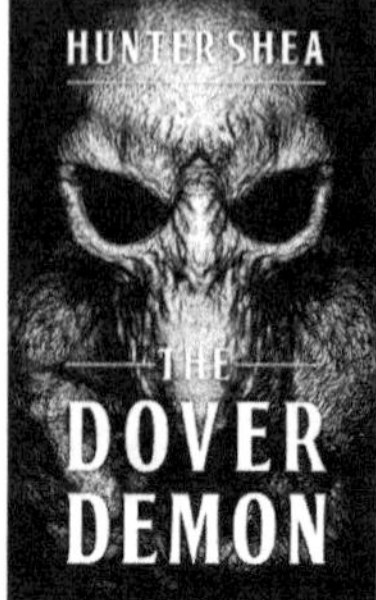

Hunter Shea

THE DOVER DEMON

The Dover Demon is real...and it has returned. In 1977, Sam Brogna and his friends came upon a terrifying, alien creature on a deserted country road. What they witnessed was so bizarre, so chilling, they swore their silence. But their lives were changed forever. Decades later, the town of Dover has been hit by a massive blizzard. Sam's son, Nicky, is drawn to search for the infamous cryptid, only to disappear into the bowels of a secret underground lair. The Dover Demon is far deadlier than anyone could have believed. And there are many of them. Can Sam and his reunited friends rescue Nicky and battle a race of creatures so powerful, so sinister, that history itself has been shaped by their secretive presence? "THE DOVER DEMON is Shea's most delightful and insidiously terrifying monster yet." – Shotgun Logic Reviews "An excellent horror novel and a strong standout in the UFO and cryptid subgenres." –Hellnotes "Non-stop action awaits those brave enough to dive into the small town of Dover, and if you're lucky, you won't see the Demon himself!" – The Scary Reviews PRAISE FOR SWAMP MONSTER MASSACRE "B-horror movie fans rejoice, Hunter Shea is here to bring you the ultimate tale of terror!" – Horror Novel Reviews "A nonstop thrill ride! I couldn't put this book down." – Cedar Hollow Horror Reviews

Armand Rosamilia

THE BEAST

The end of summer, 1986. With only a few days left until the new school year, twins Jeremy and Jack Schaffer are on very different paths. Jeremy is the geek, playing Dungeons & Dragons with friends Kathleen and Randy, while Jack is the jock, getting into trouble with his buddies. And then everything changes when neighbor Mister Higgins is killed by a wild animal in his yard. Was it a bear? There's something big lurking in the woods behind their New Jersey home.Will the police be able to solve the murder before more Middletown residents are ripped apart?

Check out other great

Cryptid Novels!

Ian Faulkner

CRYPTID

Be careful what you look for. You might just find it.1996. A group of 14 students walked into the trackless virgin forests of Graham Island, British Columbia for a three-day hike. They were never seen again. 2019. An American TV crew retrace those students' steps to attempt to solve a 23-year-old mystery.A disparate collection of characters arrives on the island. But all is not as it seems. Two of them carry dark secrets. Terrible knowledge that will mean death for some – but a fighting chance of survival for others. In the hidden depths of the forests – man is on the menu. Some mysteries should remain unsolved...

Eric S. Brown

LOCH NESS HORROR

The Order of the Eternal Light, a secret organization have foretold the end of the human race. In order to save all humanity, agents of the Order must locate the Loch Ness Monster and obtain a sample of its blood for within in it is the key to stopping the apocalypse but finding the monster will be no easy task.

www.ingramcontent.com/pod-product-compliance
Lightning Source LLC
Chambersburg PA
CBHW061243170626
46809CB00007B/2804

* 9 7 8 1 9 2 3 1 6 5 7 9 3 *